ECHOES OF THE ENGINE

ECHOES OF THE ENGINE

PARKS PAT MYSTERIES
BOOK TEN

P.D. WORKMAN

PD WORKMAN

ISBN: 9781774686478 (KDP Paperback)
ISBN: 9781774686461 (KDP Hardcover)
ISBN: 9781774686492 (Large Print)
ISBN: 9781774686515 (Lulu Paperback)
ISBN: 9781774686485 (ePub)
ISBN: 9781774686508 (Accessible Audio)

ALSO BY P.D. WORKMAN

MYSTERY/SUSPENSE:

Kenzie Kirsch Medical Thrillers

Unlawful Harvest

Doctored Death

Dosed to Death

Gentle Angel

Rushin' Death

Posed for Death

Death of a Corpse

Endowed with Death

Shattered to Death

Captured in Death

Currying Death

Healed to Death

Death's Charm

Parks Pat Mysteries
Police Procedural Set in Canada

Out with the Sunset

Long Climb to the Top

Dark Water Under the Bridge

Immersed in the View

Skimming Over the Lake

Hazard of the Hills

Knows the Hills

Spanning the Creek

Sanctuary in the Stream

Echoes of the Engine

Bench with a View

Beneath the Icy Depths

Grounded in the Wind (Coming Soon)

Reservoir of Secrets (Coming Soon)

Peril in the Blooms (Coming Soon)

Bleeding Hearts Valley Thrillers
An Abrupt Departure

High-Tech Crime Solvers Series
Virtually Harmless

Cowritten with D. D. VanDyke
California Corwin P. I. Mystery Series
The Girl in the Morgue

Stand Alone Suspense Novels
Looking Over Your Shoulder

Lion Within

Pursued by the Past

In the Tick of Time

Loose the Dogs

AND MORE AT PDWORKMAN.COM

To those who want to be seen.

STYLE NOTE

Since my largest readership is in the USA, I have chosen to use US spellings throughout this series. That includes the Americanization of centre to center, even where it is an actual place name, just for consistency's sake. I apologize to my Canadian readers for this.

I have chosen, however, to use Canadian grammar, particularly for Canadian voices. If you see what you think is a grammar error, it may just be Canadian, eh?

CHAPTER ONE

*I*t was a gorgeous day, clear, sitting at ten degrees above zero, so Margie and her daughter Christina only needed light jackets, particularly when running to keep up with Stella, who was greatly enjoying her first visit to Pearce Estate Park. The leaves of the poplar trees were a brilliant yellow, carpeting the grass and the pathways, crisp and crunchy under their feet. Margie loved the fall and, so far, the season had been mild. Calgary autumns could be beautiful and breathtaking or turn snowy and deadly. They were impossible to predict.

The slightly vinegary smell of the poplars mixed with the smoke of portable BBQs set up in the picnic areas. Everyone and his dog were out to enjoy the beautiful day.

"You're so crazy," Margie told Stella as the dog dashed ahead, pulling on the leash to smell another tree, as enthusiastic as if it had been the first she had seen in months rather than the two hundredth today.

Christina laughed and jogged to keep up with them, her long black hair flowing loose behind her. "She's so happy to be here."

They stopped and waited while Stella smelled the scent post and then dashed on to the next one. Bikes whizzed by them on the pathway, the cyclists serious, heads down and eyes straight ahead, focused on their workouts. Margie watched a family with two young children at the edge of the Bow River, pointing and throwing rocks. Their words were too distant to make out.

The ground started to shake beneath their feet. Stella stopped what she was doing and looked around, her tail tucked, worried about the new development.

"It's okay," Margie told her. "It's just a train."

"It's close," Christina observed, looking around.

"It is. It's going to cross the river up there." Margie pointed to the railway bridge stretching over the Bow River. She bent down to scratch anxious Stella's ears. "There's no need to worry, girl. It's perfectly safe."

The rumbling grew louder, and they heard the train whistle. It was a familiar sound. The rumbling transformed into the rhythmic clack of the wheels as they moved over the ties. Then, the train came into view on the bridge. Red engines at the front and varicolored boxcars stretched out in a long line.

The horn sounded again, longer and more insistent this time. Margie watched it, unconcerned. She knew the train was required to blow its horn at every crossing. The crossing at Pearce Estate Park was safe, a below-grade pedestrian crossing that dipped under the train bridge so there was no chance of an unexpected encounter between train and pedestrian. A person could stand right under the tracks as the train rumbled overhead. Though it probably wasn't a good idea with the bicycle traffic going through there. The cyclists didn't always slow down even though they could not see around the curve or down into the dip under the tracks.

Something was wrong. The wheels started to screech, dragging over the track as the brakes were applied. The train had too much weight and inertia to stop quickly. It might take a couple of kilometers to come to a complete stop if it were going fast enough.

Christina looked over her shoulder at Margie. "Why is it stopping?"

"I don't know."

"Is there a switch? Is it changing directions?"

"No. There's no switch here. I don't know why it would be stopping."

They walked closer, watching anxiously. Other park enthusiasts were stopping to look at the train as well. Clearly, Margie and Christina were not the only ones who thought it odd. It wasn't normal for the train to stop there. Margie held Stella's leash tightly as they walked up to the point where they could see the below-grade crossing. The wheels were still screeching as the train slowed and eventually ground to a halt. Then, it was suddenly too quiet. Margie gazed up at the still train, waiting. A train had two options. Forward or backward. There was no reason to stop unless it was loading or unloading and it wasn't doing that in the middle of the park.

Margie looked up the embankment to her left. There was a worn path leading up to the tracks. Not a paved pathway, but a "goat trail" people had used to climb up to look at the tracks in the past.

"Here," she held the leash out to Christina. "You stay here."

Christina frowned, shaking her head and not taking the end of the leash. "Why? What are you doing?"

"I'm just going to go up and make sure everything is okay. But I don't want Stella up there. Please take her."

Christina took the loop of the leash reluctantly. "Mom, you should just stay down here. You're not supposed to go up there."

"I know. I won't be long."

Margie climbed up the slope, ignoring the glares of the other walkers looking on. The train was too quiet. It did not start moving again, but sat on the tracks like a cooling teakettle, creaking and ticking its complaints.

Even before Margie climbed up to the level of the train, she spotted a homeless encampment in the trees to her left: a small tent, a tarp, and a bike with a trailer. Someone who had been on the skids for a while, used to fending for himself.

Margie ignored the various Warning and No Trespassing signs posted beside the tracks and continued to press forward until she could see the dark shape that was partially on and partially off the tracks. She didn't get too close, conscious of the need to preserve the scene.

While her first action should have been to check for signs of life, such an act seemed totally unnecessary under the circumstances.

CHAPTER TWO

*M*argie stood there for a moment before acting. She wasn't frozen, exactly. She knew what to do next; it just seemed ridiculous, like she was in the middle of a play or a scenario described in a textbook. She should not have been there. This should not be happening during her relaxing walk in Pearce Estate Park.

Eventually, she dialed 9-1-1. When she reached the emergency dispatcher, she identified herself as a homicide officer and did her best to describe the situation and location. In a dispassionate voice, the dispatcher ran through her script, not commenting on how unusual it was for Margie to be the one to call it in.

"A unit has been dispatched," she advised Margie. "Please stay where you are and don't touch anything. Stay well back from the train."

"Yes, I am."

"Do you want me to stay on the line with you?"

"No, I'll be fine," Margie assured her. "I'll wait for them to arrive. Can you transfer me over to the homicide unit?"

"One moment, please."

In a few seconds, there was a click and the sound of a ringing line. Margie waited for it to be picked up.

"Homicide unit, Detective Cruz."

"Cruz, it's Patenaude."

There was a pause while Cruz probably looked at his phone screen again. "Were you transferred by the emergency operator?"

"Yes. There's been an incident in Pearce Estate Park. I called it in, but I thought I would get a jump on the process before the patrol gets here to take a look and agree that it is a homicide case. Are you free? And can you call the medical examiner's office?"

"Murder?"

"Accident, I think. But we'll need everyone in on it to do their part."

"Sure. Fill me in."

Margie gave him a few sparse details, then hung up so he could do his part. She wasn't sure whether to stay at the scene or go back down the goat path to fill Christina in on what was happening. She didn't want to leave her teenage daughter down there wondering what was happening, but also needed to keep her eyes on the scene until someone else was there to help.

She tapped on Christina's name on her phone screen. Christina answered almost immediately.

"Mom? What's going on? People are kind of starting to freak out. I said everyone is just supposed to stay down here, but no one wants to listen to a kid."

"Tell them that the police are on their way and they will be in trouble if they come up here."

"The police are on their way," Christina repeated, warning those with her. "Why? What happened? Did it... break down? Was it sabotaged or something?"

"No. It stopped because it hit something. Just keep everyone there if you can. I'll explain later."

"The train hit something," Christina again announced to her audience. "The police will take care of it."

Margie could hear people complaining, demanding to know why it was a police matter. Getting restless.

"I'm sorry, Christina. I have to babysit the scene, or I would come down and help you. The police shouldn't be too long."

But of course, they couldn't get there instantly. Margie didn't have her radio, so she couldn't hear whether they had scrambled more than one unit. Whether it was a car patrolling nearby or a couple of bike cops from downtown. It was fifteen minutes before a uniformed constable climbed the goat path and joined Margie.

"You're a detective?" he asked as he approached her, black mask in place, eyes moving around restlessly to take in the scene, head on a swivel.

"Detective Margie Patenaude," she introduced herself. "Detective Pat, if you like."

"Constable Morris." His eyes went to her face as he considered her, perhaps noting the facial features she had inherited from her Cree ancestors. "Parks Pat?"

Margie rolled her eyes. "Yes, Parks Pat," she confirmed with a wry smile. "And here I am again… in another park."

"Maybe you should stop hanging around parks," he suggested seriously.

Margie chuckled. "I don't think that would actually stop homicides from occurring in the parks."

He looked as if he might doubt this, but didn't say so aloud. "So… what have we got here?"

Margie made a motion toward the figure on the ground. "It looks as though… pedestrian met train. I don't know anything more than that yet."

"Did you see it happen?"

"No. It heard the train whistle, just the usual crossing signal, and then several more warning whistles. Then it hit the brakes."

"Did you hear the impact?"

"No. The train itself is too noisy. I didn't hear any scream, or impact, or anything like that. When the train stopped, I came up to investigate. I just... had a feeling."

At that point, a man came walking down the tracks. Tall, slim, with a rough-hewn hatchet face. Wearing the train company's logo on his sleeve.

"What's going on here?" he demanded. "You can't be here," he told Margie. He didn't tell the uniformed constable the same. Apparently, he recognized his jurisdiction did not extend that far.

"Calgary Homicide," Margie introduced herself. "Can you tell me what happened?"

"You're a homicide cop? How did you get here so fast?"

"I was in the park. Came up to check things out when I saw the train stop."

The train employee looked around and grimaced, seeing the dark form caught under the train. But he didn't duck into the bushes to lose his lunch. He looked experienced and stood with that particularly tall and stiff stance that suggested he had served in the armed forces, where he might have seen his share of bloody deaths.

"This is a mess," he said grimly.

"I know," Margie agreed. "Are you... the train engineer?"

"No, he's still up there. Supposed to stay put. We can't leave the engine unattended; he will need to be ready to move the train when... when it can be moved. I'm CP Rail security."

Margie wondered whether it was usual for every train to have a security officer aboard or whether they had just lucked out in this case. She knew little about how trains or the railway police operated.

"You'll need to stay well away from the train until the forensic guys have had a look," she told him.

"I need to be a part of this investigation."

"And you will be. But I'm not messing around with the evidence, either. I'm waiting for the science guys to do their thing so I don't contaminate anything."

He grunted and scowled.

"Can you watch the scene for a moment?" Margie asked Morris. "I just need to talk to my daughter."

He nodded his agreement. "Sure." He stood with his feet apart in a wide base, his thumbs in his belt, looking solid and immovable. Margie was satisfied that he could handle anything that came up while she went back to talk to Christina.

She descended the goat path to the paved pathway, where Christina and a large number of bystanders were now waiting, watching, and speculating. A murmur went up with Margie's arrival. Constable Morris's unit was pulled over on the pathway, blocking most of it, lights still flashing, but there was a sliver of pathway to allow pedestrians and cyclists to get by it. Another cop stood at the bottom of the path to prevent anyone from going up. Morris's partner. He frowned at Margie as she descended.

"Where did you come from?"

"I called it in." Margie felt awkward, with no badge or identification to show him. She wanted to do something with her hands. "Detective Patenaude, Homicide. But I was here with my daughter and want to make sure that she is okay."

He studied her briefly, then nodded and let her pass without another word. Margie slipped past him and gave Christina a hug, quick and tight, assessing her.

"Are you okay?"

"I'm fine, Mom. It isn't like I saw anything."

"No. But it can still affect you. Your adrenaline is pumping. You know something happened."

"Yeah. So what was it? What's going on?" Christina looked around at the other people waiting for her, who were also eager to find out the details. They were nodding and murmuring their questions and encouragement.

Margie pressed her lips together. She couldn't speak for the department. She knew she needed to be careful what she said. She couldn't give anything away, yet she couldn't pretend nothing was happening.

"Well, there isn't much I can say yet. We need to conduct our investigation before I can say anything that might make it to the media. There has been an unfortunate accident. Until we know more, that's all I can say."

"The train hit someone?" Christina asked baldly.

"Well… that *may* be. But we won't know for sure what happened for some time yet."

Christina rolled her eyes. She knew how cops talked. It didn't take much to figure out that was exactly what had happened. Still, the police couldn't say anything until they had informed the next of kin and had word from the Office of the Chief Medical Examiner and the crime scene investigators who would be there shortly to gather evidence. With the involvement of the train, Margie supposed there would also be some kind of accident reconstruction team. The public would need assurances that it wouldn't happen again. Margie wasn't sure what the railway company would do to show that they had increased security and made it seem safer.

"I can't believe that happened," Christina said. "And when we were right here! It's crazy."

"I know. This wasn't what I had planned for the day. I wasn't expecting to have to deal with an incident at the park.

I was just supposed to be walking Stella and getting some fresh air."

Margie scratched Stella's ears. Stella wagged her tail hard, delighted with the attention. Margie was sure she was bored standing around.

"Why don't you take her further down the pathway for a walk? Take your time, then maybe when you get back here, I'll be able to tell you something… like how long I'll be stuck here."

"I'll just wait here." Christina looked down at Stella and reconsidered. Stella was a sweetheart, but she could be a real stinker when she got bored. "Oh, all right. But I might have to stop in Inglewood and buy pizza."

That sounded like a good idea. Margie reached for her wallet. "I'll give you some cash—"

"I don't want cash. Just e-transfer me."

Margie shook her head. "All right. Maybe get me a couple of slices, too. I don't know how long it will be before I can think about going home. I might need something to hold me over if I end up being here all day."

"All day?" Christina repeated in dismay.

"I'm sure I won't be here *all* day," Margie assured her, though she wasn't at all sure of that. "I'll update you when I know something. Just keep yourself and this furry beast occupied for a while."

Christina nodded her agreement. "Send me thirty," she advised. Margie didn't argue.

CHAPTER THREE

*C*hristina walked on with Stella. A few of the bystanders tried to get more information from Margie. She kept repeating that she couldn't tell them anything yet, but they weren't in a receptive mood and grumbled about it. Margie left Constable Miller's partner to deal with them and returned to the accident scene.

Detective Cruz wasn't far behind her. A big Filipino cop, a father with several small children, he was one of Margie's favorites on the homicide team. It seemed like nothing fazed him. He was always calm and stayed on an even keel, even in the face of the most aggravating cases.

"Detective Pat," he greeted. "Haven't we talked before about the fact that you don't need to provide your own bodies? We have plenty to do without you seeking out new cases on your own." Even though he wore a black mask, she could see the twinkle in his eye as he teased her.

"Yeah, it wasn't something I planned on. I did have other things to do today."

"Then you shouldn't be chasing after trains. Why don't you show me what you've got?"

"We don't want to get too close until the ME and crime techs have looked things over and gathered any trace evidence. But we can get enough for a glimpse."

She escorted him over to the tracks, staying well back to avoid fouling the scene any more than it already was. The railway security officer was inspecting the wheels of the train as if they might have been damaged in the accident or the sudden stop. Margie grabbed him firmly by the sleeve and pulled him back.

"Look, Mister…?"

"Williams."

"Mr. Williams. You can't wander around here. There will be a number of experts who will be inspecting the scene, and they need to be able to photograph it as is, gather trace evidence, any biological materials… You could be damaging evidence by walking around here. Why don't you go stand with Constable Miller for now?"

"This is my train. I need to check it out. I am responsible for its safety and security."

"There's nothing you can do right now except to wait. It isn't going anywhere."

Williams looked at the train and shook his head in irritation. "Stupid people! There are all kinds of warning signs. There's a safe crossing. What makes people think it's a good idea to come up here and stand on the tracks?"

"We don't know yet what happened."

"Well, look at him!" He flung a hand in the direction of the mess that had once been a living, breathing man. "What do you *think* happened?"

"I don't know yet," Margie told him calmly. "We will find out in time. One step at a time."

Of course, her opinion wasn't any different from his. The few features that were recognizable—a thick, stained overcoat, broad back, and bald pate, suggested that the homeless person who had called this encampment home had, for one reason or another, been standing or lying on the train tracks with the train approaching. Whether they would be able to figure out *why* he had done so was something she could not predict. There was a lot of work to do, but the first steps would not be hers. Her only job right now was to keep control of the scene and not let anyone like Williams contaminate it.

"Go stand over there," she ordered him firmly.

Williams looked at her for a moment, trying to decide whether to object further, and then he finally obeyed, walking over to where Constable Morris stood guard. Morris nodded to Margie, indicating, she hoped, that he would keep Williams in line.

"Not pretty," Cruz observed unnecessarily, looking at the biological matter that had been spread by the impact with the train.

Margie nodded her agreement. "How long before the OCME and the crime scene techs will be here?"

"Sounded like they would be coming right over. I don't think they are too busy today."

"Did you bring some tape with you?"

"Of course." Cruz produced a thick roll of yellow caution tape from under his jacket. They started to string a wide perimeter, eyes sharp for all of the evidence that would need to be collected or examined. Margie hoped the train had not dragged evidence for a kilometer or two down the line. It could take a very long time to process the scene.

"So what did you see and hear?" Cruz asked as they worked to loop the tape around various trees to enclose an area that encompassed the biological matter they could see, the homeless man's camp, and the top portion of the goat trail leading up to the scene, though it had probably already been trampled too many times to retrieve any useful footprints or other evidence.

"Not much. Just saw and heard the train coming over the bridge. Everything seemed perfectly normal. It whistled for the crossing. But then it started to sound its horn more than normal and hit the brakes. I didn't see or hear anything of the victim until after it had stopped and I came up here. So what happened up here… I'm afraid I can't say."

Cruz looked around at the trees and the railway track. "And no traffic cams around here."

"No. I don't think we're going to have any video or eyewitnesses. Just whatever the forensic guys can tell us."

"Well, it seems pretty clear. He was camped here," Cruz nodded toward the remains. "And for one reason or another, whether he was drunk or hallucinating or upset about something, he walked out onto the tracks as the train was approaching. He didn't move out of the way in time; the train engineer couldn't stop, and…" He shrugged.

Margie shook her head, feeling a pang of sadness at the unnecessary loss of life. If the man had just stayed away from the railway, everything would have been fine. Just like every other day when the train traveled through the park without incident.

They could hear voices approaching. Margie looked toward the goat path to see who was there, hoping it wasn't bystanders who had managed to get by Morris's partner.

She recognized Dr. Galt, a white-haired death investigator with a small white beard currently covered by a medical mask, walking up with a couple of fresh-faced crime techs who looked like children playing dress-up, not nearly old enough to have degrees in science and forensics.

Dr. Galt stopped at Constable Morris's side to check in with him. Morris took down his information, though he seemed embarrassed to do so.

"It's not like I'm *not* going to let the medical examiner's office on the scene."

"It's protocol," Galt insisted. "Always follow protocol. When the detective in charge of the case looks at the logs and sees everybody logged in and out properly, he will be happy. Not so much if it is a mess and you haven't even logged in OCME."

Morris sighed and nodded, making sure to get all of their names down.

MARGIE HAD BEEN LOST in the case and wasn't sure how much time had passed when her cell phone vibrated. She pulled it out and looked at it, even though she didn't like to be interrupted at a homicide scene. Sometimes, the reach of technology was just too far. It would be a lot easier to concentrate without the constant ringing or vibrating of her phone and the various staticky radios that kept cutting in.

She saw Christina's name on the screen and swiped it.

"Christina, hi! What time is it?" She looked down at her screen and shook her head. "Oh, I didn't realize how much time had passed. You and Stella must be bored silly."

"We've kind of run out of things to do. Do you think I could catch the bus around here somewhere and get home? It isn't far, just across the bridge. I must be able to catch the Max Purple on ninth somewhere."

"Uh... let me see if I can do something first. I'll call you back in just a minute."

Christina grumbled and hung up.

It wasn't that Christina wasn't capable of taking the bus on her own or with her dog, assuming they would allow a dog on the bus. Margie wasn't sure what the transit's policy was on dogs not certified as service animals. It wasn't even that far to walk. Christina could be home in less than an hour on foot. But she'd already been walking around for a couple of hours. She was undoubtedly tired as well as bored and Margie didn't want her getting blisters. Stella, too, was probably getting footsore. She wasn't the young pup she once was.

"Is there anyone who could drive my daughter home?" she asked the group of law enforcement officers, a lot of whom were just standing around chatting now. "It's just up Blackfoot to Southview…"

"I could do that," offered Morris, who had been relieved of his duties controlling the scene and should be heading back on to patrol. "Where is she? I didn't know you had a daughter."

"I'm not sure if she came back here or is still in Ingle-wood. She was going to get some pizza. Let me just call her back and find out."

Margie thought Christina would be delighted to have someone drive her home, but she whined when Margie told her that Constable Morris would pick her up.

"Mo-om! I'm not a little kid. I don't need someone to drive me home. I'm perfectly capable of getting there myself."

"I know you are, Christina. Of course you are. But you've been on your feet for hours already. I just thought it would be nice for you to have a ride."

"I don't need a babysitter!"

"He's not going to stay with you. He's just dropping you off."

Christina made a noise of disgust. "I don't need to be driven."

"You would rather walk and take the bus? Do you know if they'll take Stella? Or will you have to wait for the right driver who will agree to let her on?"

"Uh… some of the buses will let her on."

"All of them? Or will you have to take your chances?"

"Take my chances, I guess," Christina admitted.

"So you might be standing around for another hour waiting for a bus to take you home. Or Constable Morris could drive you."

"Okay, fine. Whatever. I'll let him drive me."

"Good. Where should he pick you up?"

"I'm just outside the pizza place."

"Which one? Inglewood Pizza?"

"Is there another one?"

Margie grinned to herself. Of course there were plenty of pizza places in Inglewood, but Christina was true to her upbringing. It could only be Inglewood Pizza.

"He'll pick you up there in five minutes."

Christina agreed and hung up. Margie reported the details to Constable Morris. Her cheeks warmed slightly at the thought that he might have heard some of Christina's complaints, and she tried to smooth it over.

"She's very independent. It isn't that she has a problem with you or anyone else, just that she likes to get around on her own, to be independent."

"Well… that's good if she's old enough," Morris said doubtfully.

Margie's cheeks burned hotter at the suggestion that she might be too permissive about what she allowed her daughter to do.

"She's sixteen," she said quickly. "She's old enough to take the bus by herself during the day."

"Oh," Morris nodded quickly. "You, uh… don't look old enough to have a daughter that age."

Margie touched her black hair, smoothing the bun she had coiled her hair into when she had realized that it was going to be a workday for her with the discovery of the human remains on the railway track. She knew that her jet-black hair and smooth skin did not give away her age, but she also wasn't as old as most parents of sixteen-year-olds.

"I had Christina when I was pretty young," she told Morris.

"Ah," he nodded. "Well, either way… I would be happy to take her home for you. It will only take a few minutes and then I'll get back on my patrol."

Margie watched Morris walk away, his own cheeks flushed pink. She knew that her blush would not show up with her brown skin. Morris's flush made him look young, barely older than a teenager. He was probably what? Twenty-two? Not that much older than Christina.

Maybe Christina would change her mind about her mother treating her like a little kid by sending Constable Morris to take her home.

CHAPTER FOUR

*M*argie walked up the length of the train. At first, she had thought that the front of the train would be just a few cars ahead of where she was. But it had continued to travel long after the initial impact. It was quite a hike to get to the front of it.

The engineer was still in the engine but, when he saw her approach, he climbed down to talk to her. He was a tall, thin man, and was very pale. He wore a uniform, but he didn't quite match the picture Margie had in her head of a train engineer. She pictured someone dirty from shoveling coal in a steam engine. But of course, the CPR train did not operate on steam, like the train Margie had ridden on at Heritage Park as a child. And even if it had, she didn't think that the train engineer was the one who shoveled the coal.

"Hi, Detective Patenaude," she introduced herself.

"I'm… Clarence Newmeyer."

"Are you okay? You're looking a little…" Margie didn't want to say he was green, but he certainly didn't look good.

"I've never had anything like this happen before," Newmeyer said. "It's a horrible situation. There are warning signs. There is a below-grade crossing. How could something like this happen?"

"I don't know. Can you tell me what you saw?"

"The company is telling me that I need to talk to a lawyer before I talk to you."

"Well… you can certainly do that if you want to. I won't try to dissuade you."

He shook his head. "I just want to get it off of my chest. I didn't do anything wrong. I followed all of the appropriate protocols. If someone thinks this happened because I was careless or did something wrong…"

"No, I don't think you did. It isn't like you can steer the thing."

He nodded at that. "I can slow or accelerate. I can sound the whistle. There isn't really anything else to do. I do my best to keep it running on schedule. Call security if I see anything suspicious, anyone hanging around the train or getting on or off who shouldn't be. It isn't like driving a car or flying an airplane."

"If you could tell me what you saw…?"

He considered for a moment and then nodded. Maybe if he got it off his chest, he would be able to sleep tonight. She could only imagine the nightmares that he would have after what he had experienced.

"I crossed the bridge over the Bow. I sounded the horn for the Pearce Estate crossing, even though there is a below-grade pedestrian crossing. There could still be deer on the rails. People trespassing on the tracks. It happens. Teenagers, usually."

Margie nodded, saying nothing. It was best if he got his whole story out without her saying anything. They could explore any details afterwards.

"I saw something dark on the rails. Thought it might be a dog. I blasted the horn a few extra times, expecting it to move. It didn't. I couldn't tell for sure what it was, but I hit the emergency brake before impact." He swallowed. "I just couldn't stop in time."

Margie nodded. "You did the best you could."

"It wasn't a dog," Newmeyer said, looking sick.

"No, I'm afraid not. A homeless man."

"What was he doing on the tracks? There are warning signs. It's a train track. Everyone knows better than to lie down on a train track."

Unless it was someone who was hoping to be hit. Or maybe the man had been drunk or stoned. Or had passed out for another reason. Diabetic, maybe. High or low blood sugar could both cause problems.

"We're going to figure out what happened," she assured him. "But you can't be held responsible for a man laying down on the tracks."

CHAPTER FIVE

*M*argie had just sat down with her morning coffee when the desk phone rang. She looked at it, not really ready to deal with any inquiries yet.

OCME.

The Office of the Chief Medical Examiner. Margie picked up the receiver. "Patenaude."

"Ah, my dear Detective Pat," Galt greeted. "How are you this fine morning?"

"Well, I would be better if I hadn't spent my day off dealing with the newly deceased." She wondered whether he had been up all night processing the remains. At least she had been able to go home to relax and sleep.

"Then maybe you should stop finding bodies yourself," Galt told her with good humor. "Leave it to others. Maybe… stay home on your days off."

"Yeah, I might have to."

"I have some preliminary information for you."

"Homeless guy was hit by a train?" Margie suggested dryly.

"In fact, no."

"What?"

"You are wrong in more than one respect."

"He wasn't killed by the train?"

"Let's start with your choice of pronoun. *He* was, in fact, not a he."

"He was transgender?" Margie asked. She supposed she should not be surprised. It was becoming a more common occurrence. Or being more openly transgender was, at least.

"No. She was not transgender. She was simply a woman."

Margie frowned, recalling what she had been able to recognize of the victim.

"But… the victim was bald."

"Yes. She was."

"Oh." Margie thought about that. "Well, I guess there is nothing to stop a woman from shaving her head. Or was she a chemo patient? Or maybe she lost her hair due to some other disease?"

"It was shaved."

"Okay, then. But she wasn't transgender?"

She wasn't sure what reason a woman would have to shave herself bald other than to appear to be male, but she could be entirely wrong on that note.

"Her clothing was, in fact, feminine."

"All I saw was the overcoat. That didn't look feminine."

"True," Galt admitted. "But that was just the overcoat, which is pretty much unisex. Her other clothing was feminine."

"Was there any identification? Do we know who we are dealing with yet?"

"We do not yet have an identification. And we do not yet have an autopsy and cause of death. It took a significant amount of time to collect as much of the remains as possible."

They had still been working on it when Margie had eventually left the site as the sky was growing dark. The railway was not happy about their traffic being held up, but there wasn't anything the police or OCME could do to hurry the evidence collection. They weren't the ones who had hit the man. Or rather, the woman.

"So, will you be able to do that today?"

"Which?" Dr. Galt asked. "Identify the body or do the autopsy?"

"Well, either. But I meant the autopsy, so that we have as much information as possible to identify the victim."

"We will do our best. At the moment, I can offer you only a general description. Woman in her late fifties, tall, heavy build, bald, blue eyes."

"Can you tell me what her hair color was before she cut it?"

"Somewhere in a dark blond to light brown range. Maybe blond as a child, darkening as an adult."

"So it would be listed as blond on her driver's license."

"Possibly."

"I'll see if we have any missing persons that match."

After finishing her conversation with Dr. Galt, Margie hung up and turned to Detective Kaitlyn Jones, whose desk was nearby and who had just sat down with her coffee. She was slightly overweight, with a round face and blond curls that were always escaping her bun and bobby pins. She and Margie had become good friends in the time since Margie had joined the department.

"We need to go through the missing persons reports again," Margie advised.

"You think we missed something? Or that it might have been called in since then? I thought they were going to flag it so that we would be told if a matching profile came up."

"We have to start over again."

"Completely? Why?"

"Because we were looking for men who were reported missing, and the victim was a woman."

Jones stared at her in shock. She shook her head. "That body must have been pretty messed up if you couldn't even tell whether it was a man or a woman."

"It was. You don't even want to know." It had been a nightmare for Dr. Galt and the death investigators to figure out how to get the remains out of the wheels of the train as efficiently and with as little damage as possible. A nightmare that Margie was pretty sure would haunt her dreams in the future. It was one of those things she had never expected to see in her career as a law enforcement officer.

It wasn't all bar fights, domestic disputes, and shootings. There were some things she would never be able to forget.

"Ugh. Gruesome," Jones observed. "I'm glad it wasn't my scene."

"Yes, you are. And if you have any sense, you will not look through the pictures on the file. Focus on the general description, and we'll see if we can find a match. Late fifties, big woman, bald or blond. Maybe homeless."

"If she's homeless, there won't be a missing person report."

"Maybe not. It's still possible that someone noticed she isn't following her normal routine, starts to wonder if something happened to her. Or there may be a much older missing person report from when she first hit the street."

"That could be tricky."

Margie nodded. She jotted a few things down on sticky notes on her desk. "I'll need to go down there again, talk to some of the other homeless in the area, see if they can tell me more about her. Name, if she has family close by, that kind of thing. They should know something about her."

"There are some churches in the area. I don't know which

of them open their doors to the needy or have outreach programs. They may be helpful."

Margie jotted it down. "Local businesses might know her. Either because she buys from them or because they didn't want her hanging around their places of business."

"You've got your work cut out for you."

Margie looked at her sideways. "Did I hear you offer to help?"

Jones laughed. "Of course I did, Detective Pat."

CHAPTER SIX

*T*here was a lot of footwork to be done if Margie were going to identify the woman who had been killed by the train. And she wanted to get it done as quickly as possible. Word would leak out as to what had happened, and there was always the possibility that family members would hear about it before being contacted by the police. That was not ideal. It was best if they heard from the police first. And best for the police investigating the death if they got the family's first reaction to the news rather than having their opinions shaped by others before talking to the detectives.

Margie figured that in the early morning, the people most likely to know the victim would be either in the coffee shops or other places serving breakfast along Ninth Avenue or in the park. Not that it was *that* early. Margie was already on her second cup of coffee herself. Christina's school day had started and most office workers were already beavering away at their work.

But there were plenty of people still around the coffee shops. Some of them were inside, lined up at the counters or busily working their phones or laptops at the small bistro tables, but many were outside, hands wrapped about their warm cups, visiting. It was a warm morning for the end of October, already five degrees above zero, but it was still chilly to stand outside for any length of time. But the homeless didn't have any choice. They couldn't stay inside for long, even as legitimate customers.

Margie scanned their faces. It stood to reason that a woman in her fifties would be best known by other women in their fifties. Some faces were covered by masks. Of those she could see, it was difficult to tell how old people were. Many were prematurely aged by hard living. Lots of time in the sun and wind, smoking, drinking, and using drugs. None of those things was conducive to keeping a young complexion.

A woman with a red toque scowled at Margie, meeting her eyes and demanding, "Who are you? And what are you doing here?"

"I'm looking for… I'm looking for help on identifying a woman who was hurt."

Some of them looked at Margie curiously, but most turned away and continued their conversations with each other, unconcerned. Did they already know who she was talking about? Maybe word had spread through the community quickly, even though OCME hadn't been able to make an identification yet.

"Trying to identify who?" the woman asked.

"There was a woman near here yesterday. Over in the park," Margie gestured in the direction of Pearce Estate Park. "I don't have a very good description yet. But it was a woman in her fifties, tall, broad-shouldered. Her head was shaved."

The woman shook her head, staring at Margie. "Her head was shaved?"

"Yes. She looked bald, but it was shaved. But I don't

know whether she usually wore a hat or a scarf or wig that covered it…"

Why would a woman shave her head just to wear a wig? Margie had not seen a wig or a hat anywhere at the accident scene. But that didn't mean that there hadn't been one. One might have been thrown into the brush or be wedged in the train somewhere. While the investigators had gathered all the evidence they could, that was no guarantee they hadn't missed something.

"I don't know any bald woman." The woman with the red toque shook her head and looked around at the others gathered there to visit, holding their coffee cups close to their bodies, cold, limbs pulled inward to keep them warmer.

There were headshakes all around.

"Sorry, honey," a man with a dark complexion and prominent lines around his mouth told Margie. He took a sip of his coffee. Teeth yellow, a couple of gaps between them. His fingernails were thick and long, a deep yellow orange. A long-time smoker. "Maybe she was new around here. But I can't think of anyone who matches that description."

"Someone who camped in the park? There was a bike with a trailer and a small tent near the train bridge."

"A woman over there? You should talk to Lewis."

Margie nodded eagerly. "Lewis? Does he normally set up camp in that direction?"

The man with the long nails nodded. "Yeah, he's usually somewhere over there. Don't know if he will be today. There were a lot of cops around there yesterday."

"Yes," Margie agreed ruefully.

He studied her. "Is this something to do with the train accident? No one is saying very much about what happened. Or…" he cleared his throat, "people are saying plenty, but none of it seems very reliable. Just speculation."

"We can't release anything yet."

"So someone was hit?" he guessed. "You're trying to figure out who so that you can contact their family?"

Margie shrugged. She didn't need to confirm or deny it. They would all assume that was the case. They'd seen it enough times before. Margie hoped they could identify the woman quickly, before word spread to the family.

"Lewis is your best bet. But it might take a while to find him. He moves around."

"Do you think he will be over here for breakfast?" Margie flicked her fingers to indicate the avenue. "Getting a hot coffee to warm himself up?"

"No, Lewis keeps to himself. He might stop in for supplies now and then, but he doesn't come around here. Get coffee grounds at the grocery store and make his own."

"Out there in the park?"

"There are ways," the man said with a chuckle. "Not everybody has a kitchen, honey."

It wasn't like Margie hadn't ever had camp coffee. Of course there were ways for Lewis to make his coffee in the bush. A small fire or camp stove, compact and easy to pack into his gear. A folding pot or tin can or cup. It wasn't rocket science.

But she wasn't looking forward to searching the park for the man. It would be easier if she could find him outside one of the coffee shops along Ninth Avenue.

"Thanks, I appreciate the information. You've been very helpful."

He nodded and sipped his coffee. "A bald woman. That's very unusual. You would think that I would have heard about that," he mused.

"There is no bald woman," the lady with the red toque insisted. "I don't know what you're talking about. We would all know if a bald woman was hanging around here."

"Well…" Margie thought about the overcoat. "Maybe

she was masquerading as a man. Was there... a man matching that description in the area?"

"Bald? There are bald men."

"A big man. Bald. Blue eyes. No beard or whiskers." Since men living on the street tended to have at least a few days' beard growth, that might stand out to them.

They exchanged looks, but no one offered anything—no bald woman masquerading as a man that they could think of. Margie would have thought that she would stand out.

"The Drop-In Center is just down there," a tiny, wizened woman offered, pointing toward downtown. "You could check with them, see if it is someone who has used their service."

"It isn't far," one of the others agreed.

"I will," Margie agreed. "That's a good idea."

But she was pretty sure that the woman camping near the railway tracks would not be using the Drop-in Center. Not until it got quite a bit colder.

"You can ask around," the man with the fingernails encouraged, "but I think if a bald woman was hanging out in this part of town or the park, we would know about it."

Margie agreed. She expressed her thanks and walked down to the next knot of people down the sidewalk, outside the next eatery.

While some people were helpful and some were not, the answers Margie got were similar to the first group. No bald-headed woman. No bald, clean-shaven man. No one could think of anyone who matched the description. There were a few churches or outreach programs to check with, but Margie wasn't sure any of them would be any help. If the people on the street didn't know the victim, chances pretty slim that she was known by the programmers at the various agencies. But Margie noted the names of the churches and programs anyway, not eliminating any of the leads she had been given.

Then she was back at the park. While the weather was still lovely, just like the day before, Margie did not enjoy her walk in the park as much as she had with Christina and Stella. The Sunday crowds were gone, and it was populated with only a few pedestrians and cyclists. Everyone back to work again.

CHAPTER SEVEN

*M*argie walked briskly to the train bridge, but kept her eyes open for any sign of Lewis and his camp as she walked. She wasn't expecting it to be obvious, but hoped to see it through the trees. But she had no such luck. It seemed that Lewis's camp was well-hidden. She reached the goat trail and climbed it once more.

No sign of the police presence. All of the yellow tape had been cleared away. Any evidence that they had found had been removed. There was no sign of the police investigation or the remains that had been spread over the area. The crime scene techs had done a very good job collecting all the human biological material.

There was no tent or bike with a trailer. No sign that anyone else had been there. The people Margie had talked to had said that Lewis camped somewhere close by. Maybe not right there, especially after the police had been there all day, but somewhere nearby.

Margie returned to the paved pathway and continued walking toward downtown, watching for any sign of Lewis's camp. It wasn't long before she reached the end of the path, which then adjoined another pathway through the residential area. Not somewhere Lewis would have wanted to camp. Not in someone's yard.

Margie returned the way she had come, walking past numerous people walking their dogs, cyclists, and a few parents with children. There was a large structure that hadn't been there when she was a kid, coming there with her cousins over summer visits to Calgary. It looked like an old ruin but, of course, it wasn't; it was new. A place that could be a castle in a kid's imagination, where families could sit on a bench and shelter from the wind to have a picnic. A couple of people were training dogs, having them jump up on the benches or other formations and walk along them for treats.

Margie stood at the edge of the "castle," peering down at the water where the dangerous, man-killing weir had once been. Replaced with the newly engineered Harvie Passage, it was now safe to boat or raft down the rapids. She could remember watching pelicans from that location. She'd never seen them anywhere else. Did they still come there, even with everything having changed so much?

Margie continued down the pathway. She had apparently missed a fork and kept walking along the river when she should have turned. It seemed like she had been walking for too long, but she wasn't sure until she reached the section of the path that ran under Blackfoot Trail. Another thing that had just been added in the last few years, allowing cyclists to continue to travel beside the river all the way to the bird sanctuary or to turn and ride parallel to Blackfoot on the new bus bridge over the very busy Deerfoot Trail, without ever having to cross traffic. She could have walked all the way home from there.

But of course, that would be silly, since her car was still in the parking lot, and she had more work to do at the office.

She stopped and looked for the pathway that would take her back to the parking lot.

"You look lost."

Margie startled. She had thought that she was alone. She hadn't seen the man standing in the shadow of the underpass, smoking a cigarette, watching her.

"Oh. You scared me."

"Sorry, ma'am."

Margie looked him over. Another rough-looking individual. Homeless or just someone who worked hard and hadn't had a chance to clean up yet?

She was pretty sure he was homeless, but it was hard to see details in the shadows.

She blew out her breath. "No, it's okay, I just didn't see you there."

"You need a hand?"

"No... I just need to find my way back to my car..."

He chuckled. "Sounds like a 'yes,' not a 'no.' Where did you leave your car?"

"In the parking lot."

"Which parking lot?"

"Pearce Estate Park. The main part, not by the Fish Hatchery."

He nodded solemnly. "Do you want me to show you the way?"

Margie hesitated. She didn't fear the man, but was still nervous about getting help from a strange man with no one there to back her up. She wished she'd at least had Stella.

"I'm harmless," the man said in amusement.

Margie forced a smile. "I'm sure you are," she laughed. "I'm just overly cautious."

"There are people around. I'm not going to do anything to you out in public. It's back this way, which is busier, more people. More witnesses." He motioned the direction Margie had come from.

Margie was embarrassed by her own reluctance to walk with him. She was a cop. She was trained in self-defense. She was not armed but, chances were, he wasn't either. The homeless in Calgary didn't generally carry. A knife, maybe, for self-protection, but it was rare for them to have firearms.

The man moved out of the shadows of the underpass. Margie gave him another quick assessment. He was both younger and cleaner than she had thought at first. She felt slightly less threatened. He wasn't a teenager, but maybe a few years younger than she was. He didn't have any bruises or other indications that he'd been in a fight or any trouble lately. Not that bruises would have indicated he was guilty of anything.

He walked toward her, and Margie stepped backward to let him pass by her with enough space between them to feel comfortable. He kept walking, then glanced back at her.

"This way. I'll show you."

Margie followed, allowing a little more space to build between them.

"I don't think I've seen you here before," the man commented.

Did he know all of the regulars? Everyone who came through the park? It didn't seem likely. But he was right that she didn't get there very often. Her walk there with Christina and Stella on Sunday had been her first trip to Pearce Estate in years.

"I used to come here years ago," she told him. "But I just recently moved to Calgary… well, a little over a year ago. But COVID, you know. I didn't get out much."

"No wonder you got lost. It's changed a lot since then."

"Well… to be fair… I'm also really good at getting lost." Margie laughed. It was an embarrassment to her. Someone with her heritage should be able to find her way around by the stars or have an inbuilt sense of true north. But both direction and distance seemed to be problematic. She could even get lost following her GPS. That took some talent.

The man laughed. Margie took a deep breath and let it out again, feeling more relaxed. There were more people around them, and she didn't think that the young man was going to do anything to hurt her. "What's your name?"

"What's yours?" he countered.

"I'm Margie." She didn't put out her hand to shake. A large number of people didn't like to shake hands since the advent of COVID protocols. She also didn't introduce herself as a homicide investigator. She was sure she could find her way back to her car on her own, but there was no reason to scare him and lose her guide.

He nodded. "Lewis."

"Oh!" Margie was taken aback. The very person she had been looking for. She was momentarily at a loss for words, unsure whether to say anything now. She stood still, trying to decide how to introduce herself or what she was doing there.

He raised his brows. "Not the usual reaction. You have a cousin Lewis who is an ax murderer?"

"No, uh… I heard your name mentioned earlier today. I was kind of…" She wasn't sure she wanted to say she was looking for him. That might spook him. People didn't like it when people were looking for them or following them. And the homeless were that much more likely to be upset by it.

"You heard my name mentioned?" He frowned. "You heard it mentioned where?" He looked up and down the pathway as if the answer might be there.

"I, uh… well, it might not have even been about you, but I was looking for someone named Lewis who some-times… has a camp out this way. Or…" she motioned, "toward the train bridge."

"Yeah?" His dark eyes bored into her. He was no longer the causal, friendly stranger that he had been. And Margie couldn't blame him for that. She would not have been pleased to hear someone else was looking for her camp either. "Why would you be looking for me?"

"I'm not actually looking for you. Not primarily, I mean. I'm trying to get a line on the woman who was up there yesterday. Where the train is."

"What woman?"

"There was a woman up there," Margie said slowly, feeling her way through it. "When the train came through."

CHAPTER EIGHT

a woman? Up there when someone was hit by the train?" Lewis asked.

Margie nodded.

Lewis frowned, thinking about it. "Why would a woman be there? Everything is set up so that people walk under the crossing. You can't get onto the tracks unless you really want to."

"I guess she was camped out there," Margie suggested.

"*She* was camped there? No. She wasn't."

"I saw her tent and bike."

He shook his head. "Not hers."

"Really? How do you know that? Unless you were there…?"

"Yeah, I was there," he said in irritation. "That was *my* camp."

"Oh… oh, I didn't realize. I thought… well, when she was first hit, I thought a homeless man had been killed. That whoever's camp it was…" She shrugged. "That you had walked onto the tracks for some reason."

He just stared at her.

"And then this morning, I talked to the medical examiner's office, and they informed me that she was a woman, not a man. So I'm trying to find her identity, asking around, and someone said to ask you, that you hung out in that area and might know her."

"What woman?" Lewis asked, brow furrowed. "It was someone I know?"

"I don't know. You're my best lead right now. She was a large woman. Tall and quite broad shoulders. And she was bald. Her head was shaved."

"A big, bald woman?" Lewis asked. "You're saying that a big, bald woman was killed up there by my camp, and you think it is someone I know."

"Yes. That's the idea."

He shook his head. "I don't know any bald women."

"Are you sure? I wonder if maybe she wore a hat or a wig normally, but it was lost when she was hit... Sometimes, in motor vehicle accidents, people are hit right out of their shoes."

"How big are you talking?"

"Uh... it was pretty hard to tell yesterday when the remains were... being recovered. The shoulders..." Margie tried to estimate, holding her hands out, envisioning the body, and then holding them up for Lewis so he could try to envision a woman with shoulders that width.

He shook his head slowly. "No. I don't think so. No one pops into mind. Most of the women I know out here are quite slim. A couple of fatter older ladies. But they are not tall. Or bald."

"She was probably in her fifties. Older than you, but not... that old."

"Plenty of old women on the street. But big women like that... no."

Margie nodded. "Okay. I don't know what she would

41

have been doing up there. Unless maybe she wanted to see you." She looked at Lewis. "You moved your stuff? Camped somewhere else last night because of the train accident and all of the cops?"

He raised his brows. "The cops stole all of my stuff. You think they would let me walk back up there and get it? After they all left, I went to see if there was still a guard there or if I could get my things, but it was all gone. They figured they could just help themselves, I guess."

"No, we thought it was you who had been killed…" Margie spoke without thinking. "The crime tech guys would have taken it all as evidence. They wouldn't have left it there."

"You thought I was killed. *You?*"

"Well… it seemed like the logical conclusion. Someone was hit by a train there, and there was a camp. We just assumed that whoever was camped there was the one who had been hit. I'm sorry. I can find out what happened to the things they took from the scene and see what I can recover for you."

"You're a cop?" He looked her over thoughtfully. "I don't know any Native cops."

Margie nodded. "There are not a lot of us around. I'm from Manitoba. I'm the only Indigenous woman in my department. I don't know how many there are in the entire Calgary Police Service. Probably only one or two others, if that."

He nodded slowly. "So you're… in what department? You patrol parks? I always wondered if those park cops are *real* cops."

"They are," Margie said. "They work for the province or the city rather than Calgary Police Services, but they are still peace officers. Carry a gun, make arrests, investigate complaints, that kind of thing."

"Where's your gun?"

"I'm not carrying one. I didn't anticipate needing one for a walk in the park or talking to people along Ninth Avenue."

"Would you really talk to them about getting my stuff back? I didn't think there was any way I would ever see any of it again."

"Yes, of course," Margie assured him. "I'm sure once they have had a chance to review it and confirmed that it didn't have anything to do with the accident or the accident victim, they will be happy to return it to the rightful owner."

"I didn't have anything to do with that woman. Whoever she was. I just slept there."

"I'll pass that along. I'm sorry that happened… you can't have had a very comfortable night."

"No," he agreed. "It's getting cold at night. Not even having a blanket or a sleeping bag…"

"Did you go to the Drop-in Center or a shelter? I understand that a few of the churches in the area might be open at night."

"No. I don't go to those places if I can help it. If it's thirty below… Last night, mostly, I just walked to keep warm. Sat on a bench if I got too tired." He stretched and rubbed his neck and shoulders. "Not the most restful night I ever had."

Margie looked for something she could offer him. Some way to make it up to him. But she couldn't think of anything other than retrieving his gear for him.

"Is there… a way I can reach you if I can get your stuff back? A phone number or a friend I can call?"

"If you get it… just put it back where it was. I'll check."

"Just leave it there?"

He nodded. "Just leave it. I'll be back."

CHAPTER NINE

ot a briefing," Jones informed Margie as she returned to her desk in the bullpen.

Margie stopped in her tracks and looked at Jones. "Really? I just got back."

"I didn't think you were going to get back in time. Yeah, they've made some progress. Want to bring everybody up to speed."

"Who's made progress?"

"OCME. And I got a possible hit on a missing person. We'll put our heads together and see if we can verify it."

"You got a hit? Why didn't you call me?"

"Things have been too crazy. We need a briefing to get everyone up to speed."

"Okay. Give me a minute to get myself together and I'll be in there."

Margie walked back to her desk, unlocked her drawer, put her handbag in, and then relocked it. She wanted to take a minute to see what had arrived in email while she had been gone and to jot down a few notes before she started to forget anything she had learned in her canvass of the neighborhood and the park. But she could see that everyone was already heading toward the briefing room. The notes she had jotted down during her interviews would have to do for the moment.

"Briefing, Patenaude," MacDonald snapped as he moved from the break room toward the briefing room with a fresh cup of coffee.

"Yes sir, on my way."

Margie stood so he would see she was doing as she was asked and not lingering at her desk. She unlocked her screen and clicked the mouse several times to get a quick view of her inbox. She only had time to skim over senders and subject lines when someone else called out that they were ready to begin. She jogged from her desk to the briefing room to enter immediately behind MacDonald. He turned and looked at her, then nodded.

As usual, briefings were "stand-up" meetings. No one took the chairs circling the boardroom table, but stood behind them, waiting for MacDonald to begin. Thinking on their feet. Staying alert. No way to nod off.

"Things are moving on the train accident," he announced. "We are getting feedback from several different directions, so let's take a few minutes to get everyone working from the same copy."

There were nods around the table.

"Patenaude, anything from your end? You've been canvassing the neighborhood."

"Uh, no, not much. There seems to be a consensus that the victim was not part of the homeless population in the area. No one could identify her. I was given the name of the fellow whose tent and campsite were next to the accident scene. We had thought it was the victim's, but it was not." Nods around the table. "And he'd like his house back," Margie added.

Muffled laughter. MacDonald looked at Patenaude.

"Are you being smart?"

Margie shook her head. "No. I talked to him briefly. He has nowhere to sleep. All of his possessions were taken by the crime techs. He spent all night walking to stay warm."

The snickers were stifled, everyone immediately serious.

MacDonald frowned. "Call FCSU and see what you can get back. Anything that isn't obviously connected with the accident, let's get it released. If they are not the victim's possessions and were just articles found nearby that have nothing to do with the accident, we have no reason to hold them."

Margie nodded. "Good. I will."

"Anything else?"

"No, sir. I understand there has been some progress from OCME and maybe a missing person report?"

He moved on, displaying the medical examiner's initial findings on the big LCD screen.

"Victim was basically mincemeat. Dr. Galt refers to massive trauma. Everyone here has seen at least one picture of the state of the body when the train stopped. The good doctor refers to multiple blunt force trauma as well as nearly being transected by the wheels. He has done a preliminary tox screen, with no alcohol or popular street drugs present. More in-depth tox screens and blood and tissue tests were forwarded to FCSU. You know those will take a while to get back."

"No drugs or alcohol?" Cruz repeated in disbelief.

"Not on the rapid screen field tests, no. They'll follow up with gas chromatograph testing, but it looks like the victim was clean."

"Then why the hell was he—or she—on the train tracks?"

"We don't know yet. We don't know the victim's medical

history, mental state, any of that. Diabetes, epilepsy, narcolepsy…? They will continue to do what tests they can on the tissue that they have. But as far as figuring out the number of blows or which direction he—she—was lying when the train struck, it is out of the question. The body hit various parts of the train and various moving parts came in contact with the body when it hit the ground."

It was probably a good thing that it wasn't a lunch meeting. Several faces around the table were looking a little green. Margie flipped absently through the pages of her notepad, her mind not registering the words on the paper.

"And the missing person report?" she prodded.

"Detective Jones," MacDonald directed, nodding at her.

"Thank you, sir. So, there were no matches late last night or early this morning when we ran the initial searches. We didn't miss anything despite not having the correct gender. But late this morning, a missing person report was filed for Sarah Thompson, age fifty-six, a large, rather eccentric woman who failed to return home last night or to answer her phone today."

"She did have a home," Margie observed, relieved she had not just been totally inept in her canvass of the homeless population in Inglewood and the park.

"She did have a home," Jones confirmed. "She was a resident of Ramsay." She paused. "For those of you who do not know, Ramsay is a neighborhood that abuts Inglewood. The average residential listings are currently $1.6 million."

Margie coughed to cover a gasp. She had been canvassing the homeless community for a woman who owned a house in the range of a million and a half dollars. No wonder none of them had recognized her from her description.

"Okay, then," she said in a strangled voice. "And what do we know about Sarah Thompson?"

"She matches the physical description down to the

shaved head. As I said, she was widely known as an eccentric. That was one of her eccentricities."

"Was another standing on train tracks?" Gagnon muttered.

He was favored with glares from MacDonald and Jones, and ducked his head, looking away again.

"We don't talk about victims that way," MacDonald said. "They are people who deserve our respect. Carry on, Detective Jones."

"Thompson was a well-respected artist. She received multiple awards. Was frequently shown in galleries both in Calgary and in other cities and countries. Her style was…" Jones's eyes dropped to her cheat sheet. "Post-modern symbology."

Everyone was silent.

"What does that look like?" Siever asked when no one else admitted to not having a clue what it meant.

"Umm… so she used a lot of bright colors, flat, with a… postmodern influence, and her works used a lot of symbolism to express her views on society."

Bright and flat and symbolic. Margie could understand that much, at least.

"Did she spend a lot of time at Pearce Estate Park?" Sergeant MacDonald asked. "She lived in the area. She was killed there. Did she wander around the park taking pictures, using a sketchpad, getting inspired in other ways?"

"The woman who reported her missing, her executive assistant, didn't suggest that she might have been at the park or have run into problems at the park. It sounded more like she was reclusive and should have been at home in her studio. We haven't started conducting interviews with her family and friends. Hopefully, one of them can tell us why she was in the park or what she might have been doing there."

"Any other areas we need to follow up on?"

"I don't think so," Jones shook her head and looked at Margie.

"No, the next thing is to talk to the next of kin. Do the death notification. Confirm her routines, if she normally walked in Pearce Estate Park or had reason to be there. Do we know next of kin? What was in the missing person report?"

"There are some distant relations. The person to be notified is this executive assistant."

"Okay. I'll go out to make the notification. Do you want to come with me?"

Detective Jones nodded and smoothed down a few locks of blond hair that were curling up. "Yes. I'll get the information together and we can go over this afternoon. She said she would stay at the house in case Thompson came back."

Margie imagined the executive assistant sitting alone in the big, quiet house, waiting for her boss's footsteps or a key turning in the door.

CHAPTER TEN

*S*ome of the houses they passed in Ramsay were spectacular. Others looked like regular bungalows built fifty or more years before. Margie guessed they were fixed up inside and were at the lower end of the market. The houses that balanced out the five-million-dollar homes to bring the average down to one and a half million.

"Unbelievable," Jones said as she looked out the window at some of the fancier houses. "Can you imagine living in something like that?"

Margie shook her head in response. "You've seen my house."

"And you haven't even seen my apartment. It's pretty basic, and I still have to budget to afford it."

"I'll bet most of these owners don't even have kids," Margie said, looking at them. "Just one or two residents, in all of that glory."

"Sitting at opposite ends of the dinner table," Jones laughed. "Using a butler to pass the salt and pepper from one end to the other."

Margie smiled. "Maybe so."

The house they pulled up to was one of the more splendid houses. Not something that had been standing there fifty years earlier, Margie decided. The owners had knocked down the previous house on the property. Or maybe two houses spread across two lots, and in their place had built up a mansion full of glittering windows. It probably cost a fortune to heat in the winter with all those windows. And to keep it cool in the summer.

But if the owner was an artist, she probably needed a lot of natural light, at least in her workroom.

They got out of the car and approached the house. They didn't need to ring the doorbell, because the door was immediately opened as they started to walk up the front sidewalk.

The woman who opened the door reminded Margie of a greyhound. Skinny, with a pointed nose, looking as though she might dash off at any moment. She waited for them, practically quivering with impatience.

"I'm Violet," she told them breathlessly. "Violet Brody. I'm the one who called it in." She wrung her hands. "Oh, I'm so worried. Nothing like this has ever happened before. Sarah likes to keep to a regular routine. She is very particular about doing everything the right way, the same way every time. She has a very strict schedule and doesn't like deviating from it. So I knew something was wrong when she didn't come home last night. But I thought maybe she had met someone, maybe stayed out for drinks. People can… have fun, can't they? She might have run into an old friend or made a new one." She paused to take a gulp of air. "It could happen."

"It's okay," Margie said soothingly, touching the woman's shoulder to try to calm her. "Why don't we go inside and sit down."

"I can't imagine what's happened to her. This just isn't like Sarah. She's always very predictable. When she didn't answer her phone, I thought maybe she was sick. That she got in late this morning and was still in bed, sick, or maybe sleeping off a hangover. I didn't know what to think, since none of that made sense. But she was human, wasn't she? People can do unexpected things."

Violet led them into a spacious great room. There was a conversation area with a fireplace, a dining room table, a kitchen counter and appliances, everything sleek, modern lines. No clutter. It looked like a showroom rather than somewhere someone actually lived. But Sarah probably had servants that kept it clean without her lifting a finger.

"Does Ms. Thompson drink?" she asked Violet. "Has anything like this happened before?"

"No, nothing like this. I've never known her to take a drop of alcohol or anything like recreational drugs. She believed in keeping her body pure and healthy. She wouldn't contaminate it with anything non-organic, let alone anything intoxicating. But I thought... I didn't know what else to think. I thought that maybe, this one time, she had indulged. People do. Even those who have strong beliefs are sometimes tempted. Slip up."

"Yes. That does happen," Margie agreed.

They already knew that Sarah hadn't had any alcohol or recreational drugs in her system. But the fact that her assistant had suspected it worried Margie. It was something that had to be followed up on.

"Let's sit down."

Most of the chairs in the conversation area looked very uncomfortable, but Margie managed to pick out a seat on the couch that wasn't bad. There was no back support, but she leaned forward with her elbows on her knees and was fine. She readjusted her mask.

"Was there anything about Sarah's behavior lately that made you think she was upset about something? That she might be tempted to drink or take something… to settle her down? Had she been behaving strangely?"

"Well, she was… no, I don't think so. I can't think of anything that had changed or was new. She was just… just *Sarah*. She could be erratic."

"I thought you said that she was predictable? That she liked to follow the same routines all the time," Jones pointed out.

"She did. She always wanted everything *just so*, but her moods were… she was a moody person. She could jump from one thought to another very abruptly and was very hard to follow sometimes. She would be talking about one thing and then would suddenly switch topics and be angry about something completely unrelated. I think… she liked routine because her brain was so… variable. It was her way of trying to keep everything on an even keel."

"Was there anything in particular that she had been upset about lately?" Margie asked.

"I don't know. She was working on a new series of paintings, but I didn't know what they were about."

"What they were about?"

Violet nodded. She paced, unable to settle herself down in one place.

"She painted *about* things. Symbols. Social issues that she felt were important. Things that she wanted her viewers to think about. They weren't just pretty pictures. They were intended to… make people think about the way they saw the world."

"Oh," Margie and Jones nodded. "I see," Margie said. "And she had started a new series of paintings to educate her audience about something, but you didn't know what."

Violet agreed. She wrung her hands some more. "I can't think what could have happened to her. She should be back here. I don't see what this has to do with her paintings or anything else. Something must have happened to her. I've been calling the hospitals, but you know, they really won't tell you anything. I always thought that was what you were supposed to do when someone was missing. Start calling the hospitals. But they just keep citing confidentiality and saying they can't talk to me about anyone who has been admitted. So, does that mean that she is in their system or not? They won't even tell me."

"Could you sit down, Miss Brody?" Margie motioned to one of the uncomfortable-looking chairs. "We need you to sit down and listen for a minute."

CHAPTER ELEVEN

*V*iolet looked at her, frozen. Maybe anticipating the reason for the request.

"What is it? What has happened?"

"Could we sit and talk?"

Violet wrung her hands again and finally alighted on a chair, looking like a bird that would take flight at the least movement from them.

"I'm afraid that something *has* happened," Margie told her gently. "I'm afraid that there was an accident yesterday, and Ms. Thompson was killed."

Violet gasped and swore and covered her mouth. She sputtered, looking for the right words. She sprang to her feet again, far from collapsing like Margie had thought that she would. She held her head between her hands, holding everything in, keeping it from exploding.

"No, this can't be true," she protested. "Oh, no. Oh, no. You don't know how awful this is. Oh, no."

"Are you sure you don't need to sit down?" Jones suggested.

Violet was back to pacing again, frenetic. Unable to keep

all of the shock and horror inside. She had to work it out physically somehow.

"No, no. Where is she? What happened? Are you sure it is even her?"

"We're pretty sure. We will need to get some DNA samples to match, if we can. To be one hundred percent sure. But Ms. Thompson was… quite unique in her appearance."

"It could be someone else. Maybe someone was pretending to be her. It could, couldn't it? If you don't have proof, you don't know for sure."

"You know that she didn't come home last night," Jones pointed out gently. "That you can't reach her today. That none of that is in keeping with her normal personality and practices. You already knew something had happened to her before you called us."

Violet wailed, holding her head. "I knew it had to be something awful. She would have been here, unless something horribly tragic had happened to her. She would always be here. Even on a night when she had a showing that went late, she was always here by ten. Like clockwork."

"She needed that routine."

"Yes." Violet sniffled and swiped at her nose. She hadn't started crying and didn't have a tissue in her hand. Margie glanced around the room for a box of tissues. She hadn't thought to bring anything in with her. Usually, she kept a purse pack of Kleenex tissues for just such an occasion. But she had assumed that there would be a box handy in a big house like this.

"What happened to her?" Violet asked with another sniffle.

"There was an accident in the park."

Violet shook her head. "What park?"

Margie had wondered whether Sarah walked there often. Whether that was part of her routine. She might go there to exercise, sketch, or get inspiration, to clear her head before or after a big project. She might consider it "her" park. Maybe she had seen the homeless encampment and had confronted Lewis, wanting to keep her park clean and pristine. Pure, like her body.

"Pearce Estate Park," Jones advised. "Did she go there often?"

"Pearce Estate Park? Over by the river? No, she didn't really like it over there. Said that it was too… urban. Too many people, too many bums. Her words, not mine. Full of sniveling little kids, bums, and cyclists who wouldn't watch where they were going."

"So she had been there," Margie observed. "But she didn't enjoy spending time there."

"She liked wilderness areas. When she needed to get back to nature, she would go on a retreat. Sometimes, between art projects, as a sort of palate cleanser. Get back to nature. Clear her head. She would go to these places that were really wild. Where there weren't a lot of computers or tourists."

"I get the feeling she didn't really like people," Margie suggested, giving Violet a little smile in the hopes of taking the edge off the question.

"Well, no. She would be the first one to tell you that, so I can't very well tell you otherwise. If I did, someone would just tell you the truth anyway. I think she liked people better than she pretended to. She could be… tender at times. She often inquired after my parents, and it wasn't just the sort of casual friendly inquiry that you are supposed to say 'fine' to and go on with the conversation. She really wanted to know. She had a lot of expectations of the people she worked with, a lot of high expectations. But if something happened… if you were sick, or had a sick kid or parent, or a death in the family, she expected you to take the time off. There was no question about it. She treated people... the way she would want to be treated, I think."

"Tough but fair?" Jones suggested.

"Yeah. She had high expectations of herself, too. It wasn't just like everyone around her was there to serve her. She wanted... for people to have expectations of her, too. To hold her to a high standard. She demanded that we always tell her exactly what we thought, whether it was about one of her paintings or something else."

"And she tried to keep her body pure, and to educate people through her art," Margie said, starting to build a picture of this woman in her mind. Tough. Hard to please. But tough on herself, too. Expecting herself to attain or surpass the standards she set for others around her.

"Yes. She was always trying to improve herself."

"Any idea why she would have been in the park?" Jones asked. "Anything you can think of that might have led her there?"

"I can't think... unless it was something about her new project. Sometimes, she had to do research at a particular location. Or to meet someone. She was very hands-on. She expected all of her work to be... authentic. Even if it was symbolic."

"I wonder if we could see some of her work," Margie suggested. "Maybe we can understand it better."

"Yes, of course," Violet agreed. "Yes, come with me and I'll take you to her studio."

Margie and Jones rose to their feet.

CHAPTER TWELVE

*J*ones and Margie followed Violet out of the great room and up the stairs to the next level. Almost the entire second floor was one open room, with windows lining each wall so that the room was awash with light even in the afternoon light of the fall. There were a few easels with current work on them. Paintings that would never be completed now. Maybe Thompson's most priceless works.

There were several clusters of gallery walls that looked like the dissected pieces of a labyrinthine maze, different sections jutting away from each other at right angles, forming intersections and corners. A painting or two was displayed on each piece of wall.

"Start over here," Violet instructed, walking over to one of the displays.

Margie and Jones studied the paintings. As Jones had explained in the briefing, they were brightly colored, flat images. Not cartoonish, exactly, but without the shading and detail Margie would have expected from a great artist. Pictures that would have worked well in a literary magazine or on the cover of the latest women's fiction offerings.

On the display walls were a number of paintings with subjects such as a tree stump, smokestacks, and dead or injured animals. Margie shifted uncomfortably. They were disturbing. Especially the ones with animals in them. Despite her upbringing in a hunting and fishing society, Margie had a very tender heart where animals were concerned. Stella was a member of her family, not a lower creature. Christina had been experimenting with vegetarianism, and Margie had not pushed too hard back against it, other than telling Christina that she needed to make sure she got all of the iron and other minerals her body needed. Margie would probably never go vegetarian herself, but she didn't mind eating mostly vegetarian meals with Christina. It was ridiculous for the two of them to make two separate meals.

"It's about… industrialization?" Jones suggested. "About the negative effects of industrialization."

Violet nodded her agreement. "Of course. It's not exactly subtle. She wanted people to understand what it was about, how she felt about the subject."

They looked at that set of paintings for a few minutes, and then Violet pointed to another collection. They all walked over to the little cluster of brightly colored paintings.

Most of them featured houses with dark windows. Some were big and empty. Others were small and in poor repair. Margie stared at them, picking out some of the other symbols in the pictures. There were a few that showed forged iron chains, thick and chunky. Others showed outstretched hands, either grasping or cupped, begging to be filled. Margie looked at Jones, who gave her a look that said, "This one is yours."

Margie grimaced, trying to decide what to say about it. "My first guess would be that this one is about… the housing market… homelessness… lack of affordable housing…?"

Violet nodded. "Not bad, detective." She seemed far

more comfortable touring them around the showroom than she had answering questions downstairs. Margie assumed it was something she had done many times before. She knew what she was doing here, on solid ground.

"But…" Margie looked around and made a small movement to indicate their surroundings. "Making a statement about the disparity between the rich and the poor and the affordability of housing for the working poor while living in a house like this…?"

Violet nodded. "She was aware of the hypocrisy. She knew her own failings, but that didn't stop her 'talking' about it in her art. Of course, when she created this series, it was before she lived here. She was in a much more modest house at that time, before she really hit it big. She went through her own struggles to reach this level of success. And she knew that… other people could not afford houses like this. That just blocks away… they are sleeping on sidewalks and in doorways."

"Or in the park," Margie suggested.

"Yes, I suppose they probably are, though I haven't been there myself to see them."

Jones gazed at the paintings. "It is a very engaging style. You want to look at it for a long time. To work out the symbolism of each individual piece as well as the overall effect."

"Yes," Violet agreed.

"How long have you been working for Ms. Thompson?"

"Oh, that's a good question… maybe… eight years. Since the divorce."

"The divorce?" Margie asked sharply. Spouses and ex-spouses were always at the top of the list of homicide suspects. "I didn't know she had been married."

"You won't find much out about it in mainstream media," Violet admitted. "She worked hard with public relations companies to neutralize any articles that mentioned Jonathan. To make sure that he didn't show up in anyone casually searching for information on Sarah."

"How do you do that?" Jones asked. "I thought that you couldn't delete anything from the internet."

"There are ways to get articles deleted, especially for someone wealthy and powerful. But even then, there are still records in archive systems. The Wayback Machine and things like that. If you know what you're looking for. But mostly, the idea is to create so much other content that anything you don't want to be revealed is pushed to the fifth or sixth page of results. No one looks past the first page or two. The top three hits comprise sixty percent of the traffic. No one looks that far into their search results, so it is effectively erased from the internet's memory."

"And she didn't want people to know she had been married?" Margie asked.

"She had a lot of choice things to say about marriage and society's expectations of women," Violet said with a shrug. "She didn't want to be seen in those traditional roles of wife or divorcee. She wanted to be seen as a strong, independent person, not burdened with all of those expectations. She didn't want to conform to gender roles."

"Is that the reason for shaving her head?" Jones suggested.

"I suppose…" Violet thought about it. "I always thought of that as 'Sarah just being Sarah,' but I guess it is all tied up into that same package. She wasn't one to do anything just because of society's expectations."

Jones nodded. "Tell us about her ex. Jonathan."

"He was a mistake. A youthful indiscretion, except that they'd gotten married. Sarah said many times that she wished that the two of them had just had a torrid affair, gotten it out of their systems, and gone their separate directions. But she had gone down the path dictated by our society and regretted it almost immediately. They were married for… twenty years? Twenty-five?"

"Wow. That long. And she regretted it the whole time?"

"To hear her tell it, yes. I don't know whether it was the truth or just bitter feelings in the end. It was messy. She said that Jonathan was just a leech, wanted all of her fame and fortune for himself."

"So instead of letting him ride the coattails of her success, she erased him," Margie said, feeling for her notepad. She needed to get a few details down on paper before she forgot anything.

Violet nodded, looking down. "There were a lot of bitter feelings, I know. But… that was Sarah. She didn't really care if people hated her. She thought we should be able to decide who we like or don't like for ourselves and not have to pretend to like and get along with everyone. That it's better to be honest about our feelings than to hide them."

Margie had seen what brutal honesty could do to a marriage. She hadn't experienced it personally, but they'd had a case not so long ago, and she could attest to how unrestrained expressions of honest feelings could tear apart a previously good relationship.

"How can we reach Jonathan?"

"I have his number on my computer. I can get it for you."

"Good." Margie nodded. "And who else should we know about who had bad feelings toward Sarah?"

"Well… I can try to get a list together."

"How many are there?"

"I don't know… a few."

A few people or a few dozen?

"I'd appreciate whatever information you could give us."

"Has she received any threats?" Jones inquired.

"Some. Not a lot."

Since most people didn't get threats, any number was significant.

"Did you keep a file? Report any of them to the police?"

"No. She said just to delete them or throw them in the trash. There would always be people who resorted to threats of violence, but she wasn't concerned anyone would actually follow through. Mostly, they were anonymous or obviously fake names."

Jones and Margie looked at each other.

Was it possible that Sarah's accident could be something other than an accident? They had been approaching it from the angle of someone who had just happened to be on the tracks when the train had come along. Maybe she hadn't been drunk or high, but maybe confused for another reason. A reaction to a medication. A psychotic break. Possibly suicidal. But was it possible that someone had intentionally killed her?

MacDonald would not like it. From the beginning, no one had seen it as anything other than a tragic accident.

"Is there anyone other than her ex-husband that we should be talking to? That had significant resentments? Do you know who was named in her will?"

Violet walked over to the next collection of paintings, frowning and staring at them like she'd never seen them before.

"I thought you said... it was an accident," Violet said. "What do you mean?"

"It was, as far as we can tell. But we need to be sure. For the sake of a thorough investigation. We need to eliminate all other possibilities."

"What kind of accident was it? I thought... maybe she tripped and fell. Or was she hit by one of those insane bikers? Or those electric scooters. Everything now has to have electricity. Power. No one can just walk anymore. Those things zip all over the place and are bound to kill someone sooner or later. Sarah hated them."

"No." Margie licked her lips and tried to think of the gentlest way to put it. There was no point in trying to keep it from Violet. It would be one of the first things that hit the news. Local celebrity killed by train. It wouldn't be possible to avoid it. "I'm afraid… it was not a scooter or a bike. Or a fall. It was a train."

"A train?" Violet repeated. "The train doesn't come this far. Only the buses go through Inglewood."

"Not the c-train," Jones clarified. "The regular train. The railway bridge that comes across the Bow in Pearce Estate Park…"

"That train? But how? It goes over the bridge. The pathway goes underneath the tracks."

"She circumvented the safety features. Climbed the hill up to the tracks."

Violet stood there with her mouth open. Everyone was quiet for a while. Margie thought that Violet needed some time and space to work through all of this. It wouldn't be easy to find that the person she had worked with for eight years had been killed in such a freakish, violent accident.

If it was an accident.

CHAPTER THIRTEEN

*M*argie went over to one of the easels with work in progress.

"So, is this one of the new series you mentioned?"

Violet walked over slowly, feet dragging as if they suddenly weighed twenty pounds each. She looked at the painting for a few minutes, as if seeing it for the first time. Margie waited, looking at the bright colors.

The cheerful tones were at odds with the subject matter. It was a portrait of an unhappy-looking male artist with slashes across it as if it had been cut with a razor blade. The slashes appeared realistic from a distance but, upon closer inspection, they were clearly brushstrokes.

"Yes," Violet agreed. "This is the new series that she was working on."

"What was it about?"

She shook her head slowly. "Sarah didn't tell me exactly what it was about. She never shared her inspirations or plans before she started a new project. She would dig in, do her research, make mock-ups and plans, and then she would paint, paint, paint, and no one was allowed to see them until she was done."

"But you could, since you were here with her."

"Well, yes, I would see what she was working on. But I didn't hang around while she was painting. I would let her work on them by herself. Keep interruptions to a minimum. I *never* commented on the paintings, never asked her about them. It was important to stay out of the way and not interrupt the process. Be invisible."

Margie nodded slowly. "Do you know who this is in the picture?"

"No. It might not be anyone. It might just be out of her imagination. She didn't usually do portraits of living people. She certainly never had anyone sit for her. She might have taken pictures of someone but, if she had," Violet looked around, "she would have it posted somewhere nearby to refer to."

"Are there others in the series?"

Violet pointed to another easel. Margie looked at the painting sitting on it. Cheerfully painted crayons, pens, and paintbrushes, all broken. Margie stood looking at it for a minute. A third easel held a canvas with only the beginnings of shapes sketched onto it. Trees in the background. Something else in the foreground that looked like pop cans and bottles.

"So... broken art tools and a slashed painting. Someone who is... destroying art?"

"I guess so. I hadn't talked to her about it. So I don't know what the inspiration was or where she was going to go with it. I wish I could tell you more, but... she didn't like to share those things before she had a final product. She didn't share ideas, only the final product. Anyone who wanted to see the inner workings..." Violet shook her head. "No one was allowed into that world."

Except for Violet herself, of course. It seemed like she kept forgetting to put herself in the equation. So the police wouldn't include her in the suspect list? Except that there was no suspect list. There was no murder case—just a woman who had died in a tragic accident.

A woman who was notorious, received plenty of threats, spoke out against social issues even though she was part of the group she was attacking, had secrets, and had an ex-husband. And the price of all of her work was about to skyrocket.

"Did Ms. Thompson have a will?"

"I guess so. I'll have to check through the files. She was very careful about documentation and filing, so I'm sure if she had a current one, it will be in the file system."

"Okay. We'll want a copy of that and the ex-husband's phone number. The names of anyone you can remember who threatened her life." Margie looked at Jones. "Am I missing anything?"

"DNA sample. Day planner, if she kept one. We should probably look at her office, if she had one here. Any medications she was on."

Margie nodded. "Yeah. All of that. Could we get her toothbrush and hairbrush?"

Violet nodded her agreement. "Yes, I can get those for you. But I don't understand why you need them to make a positive ID. There are plenty of pictures of Sarah around. You can compare them."

Margie shook her head. "Unfortunately, no. And you don't want to know the details, so you should just leave it there. We will need DNA for comparison."

Violet stood staring at her for a minute, then finally gave a single nod. "Yes. Fine. You can come upstairs to her office, her bedroom, bathroom, and look at whatever you want to. Take whatever you need."

Margie wasn't going to turn down a blanket permission. So much nicer than having to get a warrant to go through Sarah's office and personal living space. "Thank you. That's very helpful. If you want to look for that will and see if she kept any copies of any of the threats, that will be helpful and save us some time."

CHAPTER FOURTEEN

Margie uploaded the last of her notes into the shared workspace for the Thompson investigation, and looked through the various other bits of evidence that the lab had already processed. There wasn't a lot to go on yet. Some litter had been collected along with the biological matter at the accident scene, but nothing that seemed to be connected with the accident itself. Nothing that obviously belonged to Sarah Thompson. No indication that anyone else had been in the area around the time that she was killed.

Other than Lewis, the homeless man, and Margie was pretty sure that he had absolutely nothing to do with Sarah's death. There wouldn't have been any reason for him to attack her. Sarah apparently did not want to hang around anywhere there were "bums," so it was doubtful that she would have climbed that hill up to where the train was and then stayed there knowing that Lewis was around or could be back at any minute. She fought for the cause of the homeless but didn't want to be around them. Not an uncommon sentiment.

Margie called the Forensic Crime Scenes Unit to talk to them about Lewis's possessions. She didn't want him to be awake all night again, trying to keep warm and safe. He needed his gear back.

"The contents of the tent and shopping cart that were collected at the Thompson accident scene, have those all been inventoried?" she asked FCSU Investigator Dunn.

"On a preliminary basis. We haven't had a chance to go through and do any testing yet. No idea what is or isn't relevant right now."

"As it turns out, they are not the possessions of the victim. So if there isn't anything to indicate a connection with the victim or the accident, then they should be released."

"We were told that they *did* belong to the victim."

"That was when we thought that the victim was a homeless male. It seemed to make sense. But as it turns out, the victim was a rather wealthy woman who just happened to choose that place to die. She didn't live there. None of that belonged to her."

"You know who they do belong to?"

"A man named Lewis Riley."

"You got his contact information?"

"No, but I know where to take the stuff for him."

"Hmm." Dunn didn't sound too happy about the situation. "I'm all for giving the guy back his junk if it isn't related to the case. No point in us storing it here. But we like to have the owner sign a claim slip. Giving it to one of the detectives without any receipt to say that he's got it…"

"I'll sign your claim slip."

"That's really not procedure, detective."

"I know that. But we need to be reasonable about this. He can't get down there to pick it all up. I mean, he could, but he'd have to walk, and we're the ones who took it away from him in the first place. We shouldn't be putting him out to return it. And I'd have to find him, bring him in, and take him back today, because he needs somewhere to sleep tonight. It's much more reasonable for me to just take it to him."

"I suppose. If you're going to sign all of the papers. It's not policy, so you'll take all the heat if he complains or sues us."

"He's not going to do that."

"You hope not."

"I talked to the guy today. He's very reasonable. He just wants his stuff back. If he gets it back with minimal fuss, he'll be a happy camper."

"Ha." Dunn gave an unenthusiastic laugh at her unintentional pun. "Like I say, if you're willing to take all the heat, I'm fine with that. I'll say you bullied me."

Margie laughed. "Fine, you do that. I'll back you up."

"I'll see you soon, then."

Margie looked at the time on the phone and started to pack her things to leave. She would need to drive to FCSU, pick everything up, take it to Lewis's campsite, and then drive home to spend the evening with Christina, assuming she didn't have too much work to do.

"Heading home?" Cruz asked, walking by Margie's desk with a fresh cup of coffee from the breakroom. He should be going home to his wife and kiddos pretty soon, too.

"Not quite yet. I have to run over to FCSU and then the park. Hopefully, everything will be ready to pick up, and I won't have to wait."

"Good luck with that," he said cheerfully.

"Thanks," Margie laughed.

❧

THERE WAS a lot of work to sort everything out. Margie hadn't even thought about the shopping cart and how she would get it to the park. Her first thought was just to leave it behind, because the rest of the gear would fit into her little car easily. But then how was she going to carry it across the park and up the embankment to where Lewis would be expecting to find it? It was way too heavy and awkward to transport everything without the cart.

Dunn assisted in folding down the seats and emptying the trunk, which proved to be the most suitable place for the cart. He then secured the cart and trunk lid, ensuring that Margie could drive somewhat safely.

"Just go slow," he advised, "and don't go over any bumps."

Luckily, it was only a short drive to the park. Unloading everything at the park was a little easier. She carefully packed all of Lewis's possessions into the cart and little trailer, hitched the trailer to the cart, and then started to pull the whole contraption down the paved pathway to the train bridge.

She probably should not have been surprised at the glares and slurs she heard from the various park patrons she encountered when walking through the park pulling the cart despite her clean and neat appearance. No one looked past the cart. She was pulling a cart full of junk through the park and, therefore, she was a homeless person. And not just a homeless person, but a dirty Indian. Someone who was obviously just a drunk—lazy and unable to hold down a job. Her face was flaming hot. She didn't waste her time stopping to educate people. Those who reacted that way were not about to be convinced by logical arguments or evidence. They believed what they believed.

She reached the train bridge and looked up the embankment. She would probably need to take the trailer and the cart up separately. And she probably needed to unload the cart at least halfway to get it up there. It would take at least three trips, and she hoped she wouldn't end up stuck or tipping over the cart.

She unhitched the trailer and took it up the slope first, which was pretty easy. She went back down and looked at the cart.

"Give you a hand, detective?" said a voice in her ear.

Margie turned and saw Lewis standing there, smiling at her.

"Oh! I'm glad you're here. Yeah, with two of us, we can probably get it up there without unpacking everything first."

He nodded. "Much easier with two people," he agreed. He started up the embankment, grabbing the front of the cart. Margie stepped forward to grab the cart handle and push it forward. Lewis kept it from getting mired in the soft earth or stuck against any roots, and Margie kept the forward momentum. It only took a few minutes, and they had it back up under the trees where it had been before.

CHAPTER FIFTEEN

*T*hank you, Detective Pat."

Margie looked at Lewis curiously. She didn't remember introducing herself to Lewis as Detective Pat. Of course, he could have just shortened Patenaude to Pat on his own. It was a common solution for people who had problems remembering or pronouncing her last name. That was, of course, why she used Detective Pat in the first place.

But had she even introduced herself to him as Detective Patenaude? She couldn't remember telling him her name.

"You're welcome," she said with a smile. "I didn't want you to have another uncomfortable night. At least now you have time to set up before dark and to have a safe place to sleep."

"Yes. It would be nice to get *under cover* before the temperature drops too much."

Margie stared at him. Was her mind just jumping to unwarranted conclusions? Or was he trying to tell her something? She glanced around. There wasn't anyone else within earshot. They had effectively escaped the other park patrons who might have eavesdropped on them if they were still down on the paved pathway.

"Under cover?" she repeated.

Lewis chuckled. "It's not the most glamorous assignment I've ever had."

"*You're* a cop?"

He nodded. He didn't pull out a badge to prove it, but he was suddenly standing up straight, his whole demeanor changed. No longer the Lewis she had met earlier. She didn't need proof that he was who he said he was.

"After all this work, I went to get your equipment back to you," she griped to Lewis. "I just had to sign my life away to get this stuff all back. Drove here with the shopping cart sticking out of my trunk. Everyone I saw along the way, pulling the stupid cart behind me giving me the stink eye and thinking I was some shiftless, drunken Indian. Why didn't you tell me this morning you were a cop?"

He shrugged. "I needed to check you out first. Make sure you were okay. Get permission to talk to you." He looked at the cart full of his camping gear. "And I'm sorry people treated you that way." He shook his head grimly. "It really is eye-opening to see how the homeless are treated."

"I had an idea… but I had no idea."

He laughed again and nodded. "It is shocking," he said soberly. "But I have to admit, this is as good a cover as I've ever had. Nobody looks at me twice. Nobody looks at me *once*, I'm invisible."

"So what are you doing here? What are you investigating? Am I allowed to ask that?"

"You can ask, but I can't give you much of an answer. Street crimes. Drugs, mainly. But whatever else I happen to witness or overhear. Like I say, people don't even see me. They don't worry that I might be listening to their conversations. I am just a nobody."

"I'm sorry you're experiencing that," Margie said, sympathizing with his observation about the mistreatment of the indigent and homeless. "Even if it benefits your investigation."

He nodded his agreement. "It's just one of those things that I need to develop a thick skin about. I can't be worried about what people think of me or how they treat the homeless. Just be glad that I am so invisible and do the job that I've been sent here to do."

Margie nodded. She looked up at the train tracks, frowning and trying to formulate her questions. Initially, of course, she had thought that the person who had been killed by the train had been a homeless man. But that had changed when they had identified Thompson from the missing person report filed by Violet. Now, that opened up new questions. As did the fact that Lewis was an undercover cop.

"And thank you for treating me like a person when you saw me this morning," Lewis said. "I know I startled you and your instincts warned you that I might be dangerous. But you were kind and followed through on getting my equipment back for me. Not many people would have gone to such lengths."

It would have been modest of Margie to demur and say that she was sure that anyone would have done the same and that it had not been a big deal. But she knew that it wasn't true. Even most of the detectives in Homicide, who were good, moral, kindhearted people, would not have gone the extra mile to make sure that Lewis got back his camping gear so that he would have a place to sleep that night. They would brush it off and say he could go to the Drop-in Center, another shelter, or one of the churches that kept its doors open at night. Or he could wait another day or go to an outreach program that would provide him with a couple of blankets until he managed to beg, borrow, or steal what he needed to replenish his stores.

Margie shrugged uncomfortably and did her best to take the compliment gracefully. "Thank you. So… I have a question."

Lewis stared up at the sky, not looking at Margie. "What was she doing up here?"

Margie nodded. "Yes. Exactly."

"I'm afraid that I'm responsible for that." He cleared his throat and shook his head. "I don't understand why she was here that day in particular, or how she ended up in the path of the train. But she must have been here looking for me."

"So the two of you *did* know each other."

Maybe she had been in contact with Lewis on a previous project. The one on homelessness and poverty, for example.

"We were in art school together." Lewis saw the surprise in Margie's eyes. "Yeah. Believe it or not, I was once a promising young artist. On my way to becoming one of Calgary's elite creative minds, to quote the Calgary Herald Entertainment section."

Margie tried not to look too surprised at that. What had happened to change the course of Lewis's life from art to law enforcement?

"You have questions, I'm sure," Lewis acknowledged. "That's not the usual path into the police force."

"Well, no. Not exactly. What was it that changed your mind?"

He was still staring at the sky instead of looking at Margie. Deception? Or did he not want to look Margie in the eye because he felt vulnerable and exposed?

"A lot of things happened. The art scene is… quite a bit more cutthroat than you would imagine. It isn't all free-love hippie stuff. If you want to get into galleries and magazines, to have your work shown across the US and Canada, it is a lot of work, and the competition is fierce. Only a few—like Sarah Thompson—survive it."

"And the rest go into law enforcement?"

He laughed. "Well, it wasn't exactly a straight path. But after several forks in the road, that was where I ended up."

"And do you wish that you had stayed in art? Pursued those opportunities with more vigor?"

"Hell, no. I'd rather be shot than eviscerated."

Margie laughed, startled at the vehemence of his quick reply. "Okay, then. No. But you stayed in touch with Sarah Thompson?"

"No. I left the art scene and didn't see her again for years. In person, that is. I had seen her in the news, maybe even attended one of her shows in downtown Calgary, but I hadn't seen her face-to-face in many years. And then one day… she saw me here."

He spread his hands to indicate their surroundings.

"Right here?" Margie asked, back to the question of what Thompson had been doing off-trail and so close to the train tracks.

"No, not right here. In the park. I think she followed me from the streets in Inglewood after spotting me at random. An artist—she was good at recognizing people, even if I had changed a lot since we had seen each other last. She approached me. We talked a little."

"You didn't tell her you were undercover?"

"No. I probably could have, but she didn't need to know that."

"So what happened?"

"Sarah was pretty upset that I was homeless. She knew how things had gone in art school and after that when we had been trying to make a name for ourselves. That things had not worked out and I had eventually given up and gone another direction, while she had stayed in the business and been able to establish herself."

"She felt guilty about it?"

"No. She was angry. At the way that artists treated each other. We all have similar goals and should be lifting each other up instead of competing. There is an audience for all of us. Patrons don't just choose one artist to follow in exclusion of all others."

"And when her accident happened… you think she was up here looking for you?"

"I had told her that she could find me here. I didn't think she would take me up on it, but it was a nice idea, the thought of someone from back in the heydays coming up here to talk art. Maybe do a few sketches. And then I heard the train stop and saw all the police activity. Couldn't get up here without breaking my cover, so I stayed out of the way. But I was afraid from the start that it was Sarah." Lewis shook his head. "I can't figure it out. I don't know why she would be near the tracks. Unless she was… drunk or drugged or having a psychotic break. I still can't fathom what happened."

"The preliminary tox screens say that she wasn't drunk or drugged. Did she have a history of mental illness? Seizures? We'll be getting medical records now that she's been identified, but if you are aware of anything…?"

Lewis ran his fingers through his hair, making it stand up in messy waves. "Like many creative types, she struggled with her demons. I know she suffered from depression, but I don't know any diagnosed mental illness. Whether she was bipolar or schizophrenic or anything. We weren't that close. Not something that you ask someone you are only casually acquainted with."

"Well… we'll keep investigating. It might be something as simple as that. Coming up here to talk to you and then experiencing some… episode while she was waiting for you. It's not your fault."

He pressed his lips together and met her eyes for the first time. "I appreciate that. But… if not for me inviting her here, it wouldn't have happened. If she killed herself—"

"It could have happened somewhere else. She could have wandered out into traffic. Into the river. Jumped out a window or off a balcony. Have you seen her home?"

"No, never seen it. I gather it was quite something, but she never invited me over." He gave a wry smile. So even Sarah had exhibited signs of some of society's anti-poverty sentiments. She had not thought it appropriate to invite a homeless man into her house, even though they had known each other for a long time.

"Yes. It's pretty amazing. Very large, lots of windows. Nice and bright for an artist. But it could be dangerous if she is someone who experiences… breaks with reality."

"But that isn't what happened. What happened was that she came up here to see me and, after waiting for me… was hit by a train. Did she want to tell me something? To say goodbye? Ask for help?"

Margie held Lewis's gaze. "I'm going to find out what happened. But it wasn't your fault. You would have done anything you could to keep her safe. You would never have done anything that you thought would put her life in danger."

"No. I would never have done that."

CHAPTER SIXTEEN

Margie was climbing into her car when her phone started vibrating. She readjusted to pull it out of her pocket. Christina.

"Hi, sweetie. I'm just getting into the car. I'll be home in a few minutes."

"Okay, good." There was something wrong in Christina's tone of voice. Margie tried to analyze it.

"Is there something the matter? You sound funny."

"I'll see you when you get here. If you're on your way, that's easier."

She hadn't said that nothing was wrong. Margie wanted to demand to know what was going on. But as Christina had said, it would be easier face to face, when they could see each other's body language. So she would just have to wait ten minutes.

"Umm, okay. I'm just at Pearce Estate, so I won't be long. See you in a few minutes."

"See you," Christina agreed, and hung up.

Margie's stomach was a knotted mess all the way home.

She had a horrible sinking feeling that something was very wrong. Christina hadn't wanted to tell her what it was over the phone, but she needed her mother home right away. That sounded serious. Not just a homework problem. Not just asking if she could go out tonight, even though it was a school night and she knew the answer would be no.

Had Christina failed a test? Been expelled? Found out she was pregnant?

So many things could go wrong in a teenager's life. Margie wasn't late getting home, but she still felt guilty. Had she not been spending enough time with Christina? Not maintaining their relationship, so that Christina had felt like she needed to go elsewhere for attention and approval?

But Christina did want to talk to her, so that was a good sign. She wasn't just shutting Margie out. She hadn't run away.

It didn't seem like it had been that long since Margie was a teen. She remembered how she had wanted to run. How she just wanted to get out of her life and be somewhere else. She remembered feeling disconnected from her family, as if adults couldn't understand teenage problems or what she had been through. If Christina was reaching out, calling Margie, wanting to have a heart-to-heart tonight, then she wasn't at that point yet. Whatever might have happened, it was still salvageable.

Finally, the light changed to green and she could turn off of Seventeenth Avenue to Twenty-Sixth Street and then, with a couple more turns, she was home.

Christina was not standing at the door waiting for her.

Margie locked the car and dashed up to the door. When she opened it, Stella immediately started barking and ran over to see who it was. She nuzzled Margie's hand to encourage scratches and rubbed against her legs so vigorously she nearly knocked Margie down. Margie laughed and petted and scratched her to get her to settle down. Then, when she was finally calm, she turned to Christina, standing by waiting, her arms folded and a serious expression on her face.

"Okay," Margie said. "Lay it on me. What's up?"

"It's Moushoom."

Margie blinked. She held her hand over her rapidly beating heart. "What? What about Moushoom?" Her brain immediately went into catastrophizing mode, thinking of the worst things that might have happened. Topping the list, of course, was that her grandfather had died.

"I took Stella for a walk, and we stopped by to see him. But the home wouldn't let me in. They said that they couldn't tell me anything because I was not next of kin and wasn't authorized for them to give me information. So I don't know *what's* wrong. But they wouldn't let me in."

That did not put any of Margie's fears to rest. She nodded quickly and pulled out her phone. Her fingers were numb as she tried to navigate to her contacts list and find the nursing home's phone number. She kept getting the wrong buttons and having to correct her mistakes. Eventually, it was ringing through. The receptionist answered.

"This is Margie Patenaude," Margie told her in a crisp, clear voice. "I'm calling to find out what's happening with my Moushoom. Mr. Patenaude. My daughter stopped by to see him today and wasn't allowed in."

"Oh, yes. One moment, Ms. Patenaude. I will put you through to the director."

Margie had to wait while they tracked her down. Her stomach continued to do backflips as she worried about what was going on that the director needed to inform her of. Why couldn't the receptionist tell her? Was it that bad?

Christina was still standing there with her arms folded, waiting. Margie realized that Christina wouldn't be able to be a part of the conversation, and Margie would have to repeat whatever information she got back to her. She hit the speaker button and held the phone between them so that Christina could hear for herself and participate in the conversation. Christina moved closer, nodding her thanks, but still looking very serious.

"Ms. Patenaude," a nasal voice was broadcast over the speaker. Margie remembered the older woman with skirt suits and chiseled, masculine features. "I'm sorry. Thank you for holding."

"Can you tell me what's wrong? Why can't I see Moushoom?"

"I'm sorry to have to tell you this, but your grandfather is quite ill. He has pneumonia."

"Pneumonia? He was fine when we saw him two days ago."

"It came on quite suddenly."

"Is it COVID?" Margie demanded. "Delta variant? He had his first shot already. He was vaccinated."

"We have had several residents come down with COVID in the last week," the director told her. "We haven't yet put a general quarantine in place, so families can still visit their relatives who are not sick, but I think within the next week or so, we're going to see all of the nursing homes put on restrictions and no one will be able to get in."

"Does Moushoom have COVID?"

"His test isn't back yet. But I suspect so. We are monitoring him carefully. He's on oxygen. He is still waking up and responding to questions. If he gets worse, we will have him transported to the hospital. But the hospitals are overflowing; they have no rooms and very few emergency beds, so we'd rather keep him here where we know we can take good care of him and he won't be exposed to any other viruses. Of course, if you prefer that he be sent to the hospital for treatment, we will do whatever you wish."

"Okay." Margie took a deep breath. She swallowed hard, trying to keep the hot lump in her throat from bringing tears to her eyes. She looked at Christina. "I think we should probably leave him there, in his own room with the nurses that he knows. In the hospital, he would just be in a hallway, and who knows how much attention he would get. What do you think?"

Christina raised her brows, apparently surprised that her opinion was being sought. She considered Margie's question carefully, then nodded.

"Yeah. I think that's the best right now, too," she agreed.

"Okay. We'll leave him with you right now," Margie relayed to the woman. "And trust that you will know the right time for him to be sent to the hospital if he needs more care than you can provide. Please do everything you can for him. Don't just let him go because he's old."

"I understand, Ms. Patenaude. We will provide all life-saving measures we are able."

"Can we come see him?" Margie asked, though she knew very well that the answer would be no. He would be quarantined. And as the director said, the whole facility might soon be quarantined. But she wanted to make sure that Christina understood that it wasn't just because she was a minor.

"I'm sorry," the director said. "He cannot have any visitors right now. We are limiting contact as much as possible, with only one worker per shift providing care, unless he ends up needing something more extensive. The fewer people in contact with him, the less chance it will spread through the facility or that another virus will be carried in to him while he is in a weakened state. No one will be able to see him until he has all clear tests. And you will need to provide us with clear tests and proofs of vaccination before you can see him then."

"Okay. Thank you for taking such good care of him. Will you tell him we love him and would be there if we could?"

"I will have his worker pass a message on to him for you. Is there anything else we can do for you?"

"I would like Christina Patenaude's name to be added to the list of those authorized to get updates on his condition and care."

"Isn't Christina a minor?" the director asked in a disapproving tone.

"Christina is old enough to get updates on how he is doing."

"Well… okay. I will put her name on the computer. She is welcome to call in and get an update anytime."

Christina looked at Margie, her eyes swimming with tears, but a smile of appreciation.

"Thank you," Margie told the director, and she ended the call.

"Mom… thank you," Christina said, a couple of tears dripping down her cheeks.

Margie wiped them away with her thumb. "Do you have the number on your phone? Make sure you put it on. If you want to call during school because you're worried about him, do it. You heard her. You can call any time."

Christina sniffled. "Yeah. Give me the number."

Margie read it to her, and Christina tapped the number into her phone. Margie gave her a quick, tight hug. "Thank you for going to visit him. He loves seeing you and Stella, and I'm happy you go whenever you feel like it. There's no reason that you shouldn't be able to see how he's doing and, if you're worried about what they say and want to talk to me about it, you call me. We'll figure it out together."

"I didn't think you'd ask me about what to do."

"You know him as well as anyone. You've seen what kind of care they have at the nursing home. You see all of the COVID updates on the news. You're as qualified as anyone to give your opinion."

"Maarsi." Christina offered the hug this time, giving Margie a long squeeze. Then she pulled back. "We should make something for supper."

"Yes, we should," Margie agreed.

CHAPTER SEVENTEEN

*M*argie felt like they were late getting to talk to Jonathan, Sarah Thompson's ex-husband. They should have spoken to him the day that she was killed. But they didn't know who she was until the second day and only learned about Jonathan's existence later. So she had to console herself that they had tracked him down and arranged an interview with him as quickly as they could.

When she had spoken to him on the phone, Margie hadn't told him anything other than that she was a detective and wanted to talk to him about his ex-wife. He could make of that whatever he liked. She would see, when she spoke to him face-to-face, whether he already knew that she was dead.

He arranged to meet them at his home, which, though not far from his ex-wife's mansion, was very modest. Modest was what people said when they meant that it was small and old. According to the internet research Margie had done, he was an artist too, but not an artist like Sarah. He hadn't gained any recognition. As far as she could see, he hadn't done any gallery showings. He hadn't been "discovered."

He supported himself with a low-level job at a warehouse

company. They had so many made-up titles that Margie didn't know whether he was a stock boy or forklift operator. It sounded like he was in management but, from what they could find of his financial records, he certainly was not. In the retail world, a "manager" was often nothing more than a salesclerk with a few months' experience, and the same appeared to be true in the warehousing industry.

He made enough to afford the house that he lived in and little more. Maybe he had a housemate or two and could also afford to heat it, pay for internet, and drive a car. But he must have been choked when he saw what his ex-wife was making as an artist and he hadn't been granted any spousal support. As far as Margie was concerned, Sarah should have been paying for some of his expenses. She could afford it and he had suffered a lot of losses in the divorce, which did not appear to be his fault.

Jonathan's eyes were big when he answered the door. He tried to act nonchalant about a couple of police detectives coming over to visit him, but he didn't quite pull it off. It was clear that he was anxious and that talking to cops did not fall into his usual experience. He didn't wear a mask, but they did, and Margie knew some people found them menacing.

"Uh, come on in," he invited Margie and Cruz, kicking a few pairs of shoes from behind the door so that he could open it wider for them. The house was small. The blinds and curtains over the living room window made it dark. Margie could smell the previous night's dinner, or maybe breakfast, but she didn't think people should fry onions first thing in the morning. Jonathan had not thought to tidy up the living room when Margie had made arrangements to come and see him. So he had to make room for them now, picking up books, discarded clothes, remote controls, dirty dishes, and flyers turning yellow with age.

"Have a seat," Jonathan muttered. "Let me just get rid of this stuff."

He was back in a minute, having dumped everything in a pile somewhere in the kitchen. Margie didn't know whether they had ended up on the counter, kitchen table, or floor.

Jonathan sat in his easy chair. At first, he tilted it back as if he were going to watch TV, then apparently decided that was not appropriate and returned it to its upright position.

"So… exactly what is this about?" Jonathan asked. "Some kind of tax thing?"

"What makes you think that?" Margie asked neutrally.

"Well… she's making a lot of money. Maybe she isn't paying all of her taxes. I don't know."

"It isn't about taxes."

"Okay." He shrugged. "What is it about, then?"

"When was the last time you talked to Ms. Thompson?"

"I don't really know. We weren't in regular contact."

"A week, month, year?" Margie prodded.

"I guess… probably like a month."

"And what would you have been in contact with her about?"

"Just… catching up. I don't know."

"You were still friends? It was amicable?"

"Amicable?" Repeating Margie's words meant that he was stalling, trying to think his way out of the situation. Trying to sort out the best answer and anticipate her responses. "Well, I guess amicable isn't the word I would use. But I still saw her around town sometimes. We're both in the art world. There was a school reunion… maybe that was where I talked to her last." He left the statement hanging for a minute, then nodded. "Yeah, I think that was it."

"A school reunion? High school?"

"No, art school. Seeing where everyone is now, what

they're all working on, whether people ended up in art or in something else."

"Ah." Margie wondered whether Lewis had gone to that reunion. He hadn't mentioned it. Maybe Sarah had told him about it and tried to get him to go. Maybe she hadn't. "Who else saw you there?"

Jonathan's eyes widened at the implication that he needed to provide an alibi. He rubbed the bridge of his nose, thinking.

"Uh… Daniel Reynolds. Sarah. Me. A couple of our teachers were there. Other students… I don't know everyone's names. We didn't work on a lot of group projects. You really just knew whoever you hung out with. Isaac Smith. A woman, what was her name… Jenna. Can't remember her last name. The alumni people will be able to find it for you. And they must have phone numbers for people. Email addresses, locations."

Margie wrote down each of the names. "How many of you were still in art-related fields?"

"Sarah was the most successful, obviously. Daniel Reynolds, he's quite well-known. You might have heard of him?" Jonathan left his question hanging.

"No," Margie shook her head. "Is he any good?"

"He's great. Better than Sarah, but not as popular as she is. There's a joke in the art world that anything popular can't be very good. It's sort of… stuck up, I guess. A way to make those of us who are not as popular feel good about ourselves."

Margie nodded. She had heard things like that before, and she wasn't even in the art world. She never could understand the more high-brow art, or art that was supposed to be very symbolic or to shock. Sarah's work, though symbolic was, at least, recognizable enough to puzzle out the meanings if you saw enough of the pieces in the series and thought about it long enough.

"What do you know about the latest project Sarah was working on?"

"Nothing. I don't know if she told anyone else at the reunion, but she didn't tell me. She was like that. She didn't want to give too much away until it was completely finished and ready for viewing. She didn't need any outside input. She knew what she wanted and how she wanted it to look when she was done, and she went ahead and did it. She didn't have an advisory committee, a mentor, or talk to any of her friends—or exes—about it."

CHAPTER EIGHTEEN

*M*argie gave Cruz a nod, letting him move forward with his part in the discussion. He leaned forward.

"Mr. Thompson. I'm sorry to have to tell you this, but Sarah Thompson passed away recently. We are looking into her death."

"Looking into it? Does that mean it was…" He cleared his throat. They waited for him to finish his sentence. "Murder?" Jonathan finally asked.

"It initially looked like an accident," Cruz told him. "But we need to investigate all eventualities. Is there anyone that you are aware of who had a grudge against Ms. Thompson?"

Jonathan's mouth opened and closed a few times.

"Well, other than me, you mean? I guess so. Sarah never minced words. If she had a problem with someone or with their opinion, she would tell them. Some people find that refreshing. Others find it offensive."

Depending solely on whether her opinion of them was complimentary or critical, Margie assumed.

"Do you know if she had trouble with anyone in particular?"

"No. If you want to know that, I would ask that assistant of hers. Violet. She knows everything. She would be able to tell you if anyone was bothering Sarah."

"She said there had been threats, but she hadn't kept track of any of them."

Jonathan shrugged. He spread his hands apart. "I don't know any more than that. I'd heard rumors that she'd gotten threats. But Sarah wasn't the type to be cowed by someone writing poison pen letters, hiding behind anonymity. She would have been pretty disparaging about that."

"She thought that if you had something to say, you should say it face-to-face and not mince words," Margie suggested.

"Yes, exactly. But she wasn't a mean person. There were plenty of times when she just kept her mouth shut and didn't say anything. She wasn't one to run down other artists' work; I'll say that for her. I never heard her say a derogatory word about someone else's work. And believe me, we had plenty of opportunities in school to critique each other's work. Sarah was always very professional about it. Others in the class… never did get the hang of critiquing without it sounding like a personal attack."

After Lewis's comments about how cutthroat the industry could be, Margie could understand what he was talking about. She pondered the new series of paintings Sarah had been working on. A slashed canvas of an unhappy artist. Broken art implements. Could the series have been about someone destroying an artist with unfair criticism or personal attacks?

"Do you know of anyone who had criticized Sarah that way?"

"Recently?" Jonathan considered for a moment, then shook his head. "No. But there's always criticism in the art world. The more you're in the spotlight, the more people will be jealous and make personal attacks. Hold you up as the worst representative in your genre."

"And with the internet, it is easier than ever to get the word out," Cruz said, "and still hide behind anonymity."

Jonathan looked in his direction and didn't agree or disagree. Margie thought she detected a red flush around his throat. Maybe he'd been more involved in attacks against his ex-wife than he wanted them to know about.

"Where were you Sunday afternoon?" she asked Jonathan.

"Sunday?" Jonathan stalled, repeating the question and scratching the back of his head as if it were a difficult question to answer. "Gee... I don't know. I lose track of what day it is..."

"You work. Was it a workday?"

"No. I never work on a Sunday."

"So you weren't working. What did you do on the weekend?"

He swallowed, still considering the question. "Is that when she died? Is that why you're asking? You think that I was involved somehow in this accident, and you want to see if I have an alibi?"

"We are investigating your ex-wife's death. We would like to know where you were when she died," Cruz said in his tough-cop voice.

Margie kept her face expressionless, but she was inwardly amused. Cruz put on a good tough-guy act, but she knew he was a family man, compassionate, even-tempered, and abhorred violence.

That didn't mean he couldn't handle himself if a situation required it. He was just as good with a gun or methods of subduing a violent offender as anyone else in the department. But it wasn't like on TV. No one was going to take Jonathan into a room lit by a single bulb and beat him until he confessed.

"I was… at an art show. Downtown. One of the guys in our class. Isaac. Isaac Smith. You can look it up. The gallery will tell you he had a show."

"Will the gallery be able to confirm that you were there?" Margie asked.

"Well… not the gallery. I didn't introduce myself to the owners."

"But Isaac can confirm it."

"I don't know. I said 'hi' to him, but he was busy with a lot of other people—potential buyers or patrons. So, I wasn't his focus. I waited a while for the others to show up, but no one else did. I had a few drinks, some crackers and, eventually, went home. I had work of my own to do. I still paint, but I can't do it when I'm at work, obviously, so I have to fit it in evenings and weekends."

"What others?" Cruz asked.

"What?"

"You said you were waiting for the others, but they didn't come."

"Oh. Some of the others from the art class. We had talked about going together. Or meeting up there, rather. But I waited around for them, and they didn't show. I thought that we would all talk to Isaac at the same time, congratulate him, tell him what a good job he did. You know, give him a boost. But the others didn't show up, so I just… I just left without really spending any time talking to him. I didn't want to interrupt his conversations with people who might actually buy his art. Because I wasn't going to be buying any of it."

"Who else from your class was supposed to be there?"

"Sarah, of course, but I never thought she would show up. Especially not when I was planning to be there. She didn't exactly want to hang out with me. Uh. Jenna what's-her-name. Daniel Reynolds."

"Sounds like you guys were the core group from your class."

"Well, the classes weren't huge. You got to know the people that you did projects with. Yeah, I guess we were kind of 'the gang.' We did stuff with others. Invited them along. But it was usually me and Sarah, Daniel, and a couple of other people that I've kind of lost touch with."

"So they could tell us that you were all supposed to meet up at the gallery… but not that you were there, since they didn't show up."

Daniel's mouth twisted into a scowl. "I can't help if they didn't show up. They were *supposed* to."

"Sarah was supposed to be there?"

"Like I said, she was supposed to be, but I wasn't surprised that she wasn't. She had better things to do than to hang out with losers like us."

"Did she give you any explanation? Call you and let you know that she was going to be somewhere else?"

"Not me. Maybe she contacted one of the others. She wouldn't have called me."

Instead of being at the art show, Sarah had been in the park, looking for Lewis. Ending up on the tracks as the train came across the bridge too fast to stop in time. Had someone set her up? Jonathan could have intended for the opening to be his alibi, shown up there, made an appearance, and then gone to the park to meet Sarah. He could have taken one of the motorized scooters that were rented out downtown and made it to the park very quickly.

"Do you have phone numbers for Isaac and the other art students who were supposed to be there?"

Jonathan shook his head, but when he opened his mouth to say that he didn't have the information or they could find it themselves, he changed his mind. "Yeah… if you give me a few minutes, I can find something for you. Some of them I might only have email addresses for, not a phone number."

"Whatever you have would be good."

CHAPTER NINETEEN

*M*argie had a number of notes that needed to be transcribed from her notepad and expounded on in her reports saved to the workspace on the server for Sarah Thompson's file. She frowned as she worked through them, trying to make all the necessary connections.

"You ready to close on the Thompson death?" MacDonald questioned, standing in front of Margie's desk with a fresh cup of coffee. She was used to being called into his office if he had any questions about a case. Hovering over her was not his usual practice.

"Uh… well, things aren't quite as straightforward as they looked initially."

Margie had to look way up at her sergeant. He ran a hand over his close-cropped gray hair.

"A woman lying on the tracks was run over by a train. How is that anything other than an accident? Or suicide? You should be able to clear it pretty quickly. We're getting calls from reporters and people in the art world. She was quite the big name, as it turns out."

"Well, we are pursuing it. Interviewing acquaintances,

getting the details nailed down. I'm sure the people asking for information and updates wouldn't want us just to ignore any red flags and sweep it under the rug."

"Of course not," MacDonald agreed with a scowl. "What makes you think that it was anything other than an accident?"

"It could still be… but some things concern me. She was getting threats. She was a local celebrity in the art world, and I guess there was a lot of competition. A lot of people who probably would have liked her out of the way. And there is a bitter ex-husband living in a hovel, while she lives in a huge mansion. She didn't change her will after getting divorced."

MacDonald opened his mouth to counter this point, but Margie raised her hand. "I know that the divorce means that the provisions she made for the ex in her will are revoked, but that doesn't mean the ex knows that. He may think that he's now due a pretty good nest egg."

"Okay," MacDonald nodded at this. "Fair enough. Most people don't know enough about Alberta estate law to know how that works."

"The ex does not have a good alibi. But we also don't know who has been making threats—whether it was him or someone else, or several other people. Like you say, she's quite well-known in the art world, and I'm sure that has caused some jealousies."

"Are you trying to track those down?"

Margie looked at her screen. "It's on my list. The personal assistant should be able to help with that, but she says that Thompson always just told her to delete or garbage any threats, so we only have her memory to work from, or if they were received in email and are still in the trash folder."

"Is there any indication that it was homicide rather than an accident? Other than the fact that people had made threats and there is a lot of money to be divvied between people now."

"The question of what she was doing on the tracks in the first place. The train engineer puts her lying down on the tracks, not standing on them. ME says that there was no alcohol or drugs in her system. Her medical records say that she didn't have epilepsy or diabetes or something that would conceivably make her fall or lay down on the tracks."

"But she did battle depression."

"Right. So, it's possible that she was suicidal. But she didn't go out there to commit suicide."

MacDonald shifted his stance and took a drink from his mug.

"And just how do you know that?"

"The homeless guy whose gear was at the scene. They were old friends. Went to art school together. Then the homeless guy—who is actually an undercover, by the way—ran into her one day, so she knew where he camped out. She went out there to talk to him, not to commit suicide."

"You can't know her purpose for going there."

"No. But why would she go to her friend's campsite, his 'home' to commit suicide? She went there because she wanted to talk to him about something. And then... something happened. I'm not sure what that was. But something made her change from visiting an old friend to lying on the tracks."

"The homeless guy is undercover?"

Margie nodded. "He didn't break cover to tell anyone. But when I went back there with his gear, we talked. He doesn't know why she went to see him."

"But he didn't see what happened?"

"No."

"And he didn't see anything at the scene to make him think that it was murder or suicide."

"No. He wasn't there until it was all cleaned up."

"Okay…" MacDonald stared off into space for a few seconds. "Continue with your investigation. Keep me informed. In ninety percent of these cases… it's the spouse or the ex."

"I know. I'm looking at him."

MacDonald nodded and headed back toward his office.

Jones looked over at Margie from her desk. "These background searches are interesting."

Margie blinked and looked over at her. "What? Which one? Sarah's ex?"

"His is pretty innocuous. He's not very well-known. No one is showing his stuff. He just dabbles. Posts in some art discussion groups. And works in a warehouse. But one of the other ones that you had on the list… Daniel Reynolds, he's a different story."

"What did you find on him?"

"He has criminal charges for art theft and fraud, for starters. When I look for deeper background, it's interesting…"

Margie stood up and walked over to Jones's desk to look over her shoulder. "What's interesting?"

"Well, he's got lots of good press. Like Jonathan said, he's well-known, though not as much as Sarah. He doesn't have a distinctive style, but is known for being able to pull off a lot of different looks. I guess that wins and loses him points. Anyway, a good amount of positive press. But when you start looking for stuff that has been buried, you start to get a different picture."

"Like Sarah burying her divorce?"

Jones nodded.

Margie leaned in to read the small print on the screen. They were not major news sources. A few posts buried here and there in social media. A small website that specialized in exposing art forgery. Little snippets of conversation that had taken place over the years and been buried by Daniel's more successful projects.

"Maybe it isn't the same Daniel Reynolds," she said. "There might be a few of them around."

Jones clicked on one of the articles and, when it expanded across the screen, Margie could see it was the same face, albeit somewhat younger. She skimmed through the information on the screen. "He was accused of copying or stealing other people's work while he was at school?"

Jones nodded. "Exactly. He pleaded ignorance to the school administrators. He said that he was just copying other people's work to learn, which is a long tradition of artists. And that he hadn't intended to pass off anyone else's work as his own. He just wanted to see how it was judged if both his work and someone else's were submitted at the same time. Something about exposing biases."

"So it was all a mistake. They just misunderstood his intentions. He wasn't trying to pass off anyone else's work as his own."

"That's right," Jones agreed with a grin.

"Interesting. Is there anything about whose work he was 'borrowing' or learning from?"

"Not really. I got the impression that they didn't want to bring anyone else's names into it in case they got tarred with the same brush as Reynolds. Anyway, it sounds like he has some wealthy relatives, and things were smoothed over, and even though he lost his scholarship and was cited with 'code of conduct' demerits, he was allowed to stay in school and finish his degree."

"And then went on to become a successful, well-known artist. Left all of that nasty business behind."

"I guess no one held it against him. He was just young and foolish and learned the error of his ways."

"I'll bet."

Margie looked at Jones's search page when she clicked back to it, and made a couple of notes. "Can you save those to the workspace?"

"Sure, of course."

"I'm going to do a little bit more digging…"

Margie returned to her seat and thought about what searches might get her to the next step. Looking at her list of names, she decided to pair them together in a few searches. The media outlet that had published the story that she and Jones had looked at together had refrained from listing anyone else's name in the article, but other sites might not have been so careful. A combined search might tell her if any other art school students had been targets of Reynolds's fraudulent activities.

She started plugging in "Daniel Reynolds and Sarah Thompson," "Daniel Reynolds and Isaac Smith," and so on through the various names on her list.

No hits on any of them. Either Reynolds had been stealing from other artists further afield, or everyone had agreed to leave the other names out of the story.

Remembering that Lewis had said that he and Sarah went to school together, Margie keyed in "Daniel Reynolds and Lewis Riley."

There were a few hits. A couple of them just seemed to be articles where the two of them were mentioned as participants in a show or recipients of scholarships. Margie saw pictures of the two of them across the top row with others from their program.

Margie clicked on a Calgary Herald article praising Lewis's work, saying he was on his way to becoming one of Calgary's elite creative minds. Margie smiled, remembering Lewis quoting that line proudly. But then something had happened. The cutthroat business had been too much for him, and he had diverted to a career in law enforcement instead.

The same article was not nearly as complimentary toward Daniel Reynolds, saying he was derivative, uninspired, and lacking natural talent.

Looking for anything else related to the article, Margie found a social media thread with commentary on the article. Most of the posts were by Reynolds himself, decrying the article and the biases of the reporter. He not only pumped up his own work, giving quotes from various other sources who thought he was the best thing since sliced bread, but also denigrated Lewis's work. He did more than critique it professionally, as Jonathan said they were encouraged to do. Instead, Reynolds went way overboard, cutting down Lewis's work, him as a person, his ancestry, and anyone who might dare to have an opinion that conflicted with his.

> Far from being an up-and-comer or having any creative talent, Lewis Riley is stuck in the last century, as was the author of the article. Lewis's work, produced after many long hours of blood, sweat, and tears, looks like something a five-year-old could have drawn with a box of crayons. The reporter is clearly enamored with his long and respected heritage in one of Calgary's "royal" families. The Rileys may have been artists in days of yore, but what have they done lately? Lewis's insipid works with little form or substance, will not cut it. Lewis should get out of the program while he can still save face.

Margie winced and shook her head. "Look at this," she told Jones. "Now, if Lewis Riley had killed Daniel Reynolds, I might understand it..."

Detective Jones hung over Margie's shoulder this time,

slowly shaking her head. "Ouch! I'm surprised they let him post something like that and didn't delete it."

"Some groups or boards don't have very much moderation. People can pretty much post whatever they want."

"If I was Reynolds, I would probably have deleted this post later. I certainly wouldn't leave it like that."

"He may have completely forgotten about it. Especially if it had the hoped-for effect of getting Lewis out of the class and into another career."

"Did it?"

"Yeah, he's the undercover. He went into law enforcement, and he told me that he left the art world for this very reason," Margie flicked a finger at the monitor. "Because it is too cutthroat."

"I always thought that art was all… creative touchy-feely. I didn't think it was competitive like this."

"It probably depends on whether you are trying to get ahead or just make nice pictures. If they are fighting over a few sweet gigs and are afraid that someone else is getting ahead…"

But she had to admit that it was over-the-top and shocking. She would not have expected such venom between two young artists.

"The question is, then, if there is any connection between this nastiness and Thompson's death. I can't see a straight line between them."

"No," Margie agreed, studying the words on her screen. "Not yet."

CHAPTER TWENTY

Margie and Christina were working together to get dinner on the table, Margie chopping vegetables with her head in the clouds, working through the puzzling case.

"Mom?"

"Hmm?" Margie looked at Christina, aware she had missed some part of the earlier conversation. "I'm sorry, I was thinking about something else. What was that?"

"That cop that drove me back here on Sunday. What was his name?"

"Oh…" Margie thought back, trying to remember back that far. What had been the name of the young constable? "I think Morris? I remember associating it with that old detective series. I think it was Constable Morris."

"How would I get ahold of him if I wanted to thank him for dropping me off?"

"I don't think you need to do that. He was happy to be able to get away from the scene, I think. And it doesn't hurt to be escorting such a lovely young lady."

Christina rolled her eyes. "Still, he was very nice. I think I should thank him for helping me out. You always say to be polite, and I was kind of cranky that day, after having to wait around and then having to be driven by someone I didn't know, like a little kid."

Margie turned her head to look at her daughter, a smile spreading across her face.

"I thought you already had a boyfriend."

"Mo-om! Tracy isn't my boyfriend. He's just… a friend."

"Who is a boy."

"Yeah, well, you told me I should never judge someone by their gender. I should see what kind of a person they really are inside. What does it matter if he is a boy?"

Margie had been concerned with how close the two friends were, and the level of physical intimacy between them when Margie was not around to supervise. On the one hand, she was happy to hear that Christina and Tracy were "just friends," but, on the other hand, Christina could be lying about that. There was no way to know unless she actually saw something between them, and they had been careful not to let her catch them so far.

And regardless of whether she and Tracy were involved, Christina was now showing interest in someone else. A man who was not the same age as she was, but several years older. The fact that he was a cop did not make Margie feel better. She knew plenty of cops who were reckless and willing to break the rules. A lot of adrenaline junkies who loved to take risks and feel that rush. The risk of breaking the law and getting caught was a thrill.

"I'll see if I can find his number," Margie told Christina, though she had no intention whatsoever of doing so.

Margie dumped the vegetables into the hot pan, where they sizzled and released their enticing aromas.

"I could just call the main police number," Christina pointed out.

Checkmate. Christina wasn't fooled. Now that Margie had given up Morris's name, there was nothing she could do to stop Christina from making such a call.

"How is your homework coming along?" Margie asked, trying to distract her from the conversation about Morris.

Christina grimaced. "It's just fine," she said. "I'll get it done."

"I know. You've been doing pretty well in all of your classes." She was grateful to Tracy for the help he gave Christina with her homework. Her marks had gone up since getting to know him. "And how about the Indigenous Fair?"

Christina chewed on her thumbnail. "What if Moushoom doesn't get better in time to take part? I really wanted him to help out. To do some of the jigging and chanting... storytelling, talking about his residential school days, stuff like that."

"We have to be more concerned about his health than whether he can do the fair or not."

"I know," Christina agreed quickly. "I wouldn't want him to try to do it when he's sick. That's why I asked if you thought he would be well in time. I just... I want him to get better. And I want him to be able to go to the fair. But if he can't help, that's okay. I have some other dancers. I really want people to get to know him, though. He's so cool."

"I'm sure everyone would love to meet him." Margie sighed. "Right now, I'm just hoping they don't shut the schools down again. They keep saying that they won't, but there are so many kids and teachers going down with COVID that I don't see how they can keep ignoring it."

"They're not ignoring it. We still have to wear masks and not sit too close together."

"But as soon as you're out of school, you take your masks off anyway."

Christina smirked and shrugged. "And if they shut down the schools, do you think we are going to stop seeing each other?"

"We're lucky not to have had quarantines enforced by the military like they did in some other countries."

"I know. But maybe if they'd done it that way, we wouldn't have Delta now." Christina shrugged. "People are so tired of restrictions. They just don't want to do it anymore. Nobody wants to keep masking and social distancing."

"Yeah. I know. I see it every day."

"Moushoom sent his love," Christina said suddenly, her tone brightening. "I forgot I didn't tell you yet!"

"You talked to him?"

"No, but the nurse gave him our message and he sent one back. He said that he loves both of us, and we're supposed to 'be true to ourselves.'" She smiled, eyes sparkling. "That sounds like him, doesn't it?"

It would figure that Moushoom would be more concerned about giving his granddaughters advice about how to live their lives than he would be about his own health and what his chances of survival were as an old man with pneumonia and COVID.

"So what does that mean?" Margie asked, curious what Christina would come up with. "What does it mean to you?"

"Just… I don't know. Make the family proud. Be strong and make the right choices; don't let other people talk you into making bad ones."

Margie nodded. That was a good answer. "People can really do each other a lot of harm with their words," she observed, thinking about Reynolds and the damage he had done to Lewis's art career. And about the other people involved in the case and the choices they had made. Sarah, advocating for the poor while she lived in a mansion and her ex-husband lived paycheck to paycheck in a dump. Acting as if she cared about what had happened to Lewis, but what had she done to help him? Had she intended to do something concrete to give an old friend a hand up? Or was that just talk? Why had she gone to visit him the day she died?

CHAPTER TWENTY-ONE

*D*aniel Reynolds looked like he did in the news articles and internet searches they had done. A little older, maybe, but he wasn't a fifty-year-old trying to appear in the media as if he were twenty or thirty years younger. His face was narrower and more wrinkled, and his short sideburns a little grayer. But still easily recognizable from his PR materials.

"I'm not sure exactly what I'm doing here," Reynolds said as he was led to an interview room and sat at the table. He looked around the bare room, eyes eventually returning to Margie. "From what I can understand, you are looking into the death of Sarah Thompson. That's great, but… I thought it was an accident, and I don't know what insight you think I might have into it. Sarah and I met for cocktails occasionally, of course. Ran into each other at some of the same boring fundraisers, but we weren't close."

"Were you close with anyone in your old art class?" Margie asked, ignoring his pompous manner.

"Close…? No, not really. I do run into some of them from time to time, but we haven't stayed close friends. There were a lot of… a lot of different personalities. Artistic temperaments. They lead to some clashes. I'm sure you know what I mean. Creative types can sometimes act like toddlers."

Margie chuckled at the image of the artists she had met on the case, envisioning them as toddlers, perhaps bopping each other over the head with big foam bats.

It was better than envisioning Reynolds or one of the others hitting Sarah over the head with a blunt object and leaving her on the tracks unconscious.

"So, you saw Thompson sometimes. Who else?"

He shook his head. "I really don't know. I guess her ex, Jonathan. Sometimes Jenna or one of the others. Isaac just had a showing, but I wasn't able to get to it. Last-minute emergencies, you know. Smoothing out issues with my own shows and public relations."

"You didn't make it to Isaac Smith's show? I thought that you and some of the others had planned to be there together as a show of support."

"I was supposed to be there but, at the last minute, I couldn't make it."

"But you have someone who can testify as to where you were? You were working with someone else on an upcoming show."

"Well," his brows drew down and he shifted slightly. His chair wobbled a little and he moved again in irritation. "I didn't say that I was with someone else. There was a lot to be done and, as an artist in today's world, you really need to be your own manager, ready to step up and take control when things go off the rails."

He licked dry lips and looked concerned. "Off the rails— I mean—when things don't go the way you had planned."

He clearly didn't want her to think he was making light of what had happened to Sarah. An allusion to railway tracks might not be appropriate.

"So you don't have someone who can verify where you were at the time you had been expected at Isaac's show?" Margie deliberately did not refer to the time of Sarah's death.

"Uh… I was at home. There was a lot to do. I couldn't really go out. But I didn't have anyone else… I don't have an administrative assistant like Violet."

"Oh, you know Violet?"

"Sure, sure. She'd been with Sarah for eight years. Violet was the best option if you wanted to get in touch with Sarah. She ran a tight ship."

"We noticed that you've had a number of calls with her when we pulled phone logs."

He looked left and right. "Calls with Sarah? No…"

"Calls with Violet."

"Well, sure. Like I said, she ran things. She was the person to talk to."

"And she was the only person with access to Sarah's work in progress. So that you could keep track of what she was working on."

"Sarah never shared her work before it was complete. She was very adamant about that."

"So I understand. So the only way to know what she was working on was through her employee."

"I never talked to Violet."

"I thought you just said that you talked to her when you wanted to get in touch with Sarah. She ran Sarah's schedule."

"Um, yeah. That's what I mean. Just to talk to Sarah or meet with her. I never have asked Violet anything about Sarah's work in progress."

"Is that what Violet will tell us?"

Of course, Violet had already said that she never told anyone about what Sarah was working on. But when people said things like that, they just meant that they limited the number of people they told about it. What were the odds that Violet had actually been able to keep her mouth shut about Sarah's latest project? And what were the chances that the calls between Reynolds and Violet were just to set up meetings with Sarah?

Margie figured Violet would be singing a different tune when she was brought in to have a serious chat in the CPS Homicide offices about her involvement with Reynolds. It was something that made most people pretty anxious. They tended to want to unburden themselves and straighten out any misunderstandings.

Reynolds cleared his throat and licked his lips again.

"Can I get you a glass of water?" Margie offered.

He said no, but right after that, he nodded his head. Margie went to the breakroom to fetch a glass of water for him, then returned. She sat down at the table.

"So no one can vouch for where you were or what you were doing when your friends were expecting you at the show."

"They really aren't my friends."

"No. I gathered that. It didn't seem like any of you liked each other very much. I'm surprised you still planned to do things together, like supporting Isaac at his show."

"Well... it's the nice thing to do. Being a supportive friend."

"Probably not your idea. I understand. What did you think of Isaac's work?"

"Well, considering his training and how long he has been trying to break out... I expected more from him. It was all very basic. Not really any more... elevated than it was when we were in school. And that was a long time. I guess his persistence paid off, because I don't think it was his talent."

"Did you tell him your opinion?"

Reynolds hesitated. "He didn't ask me my opinion. I try to be honest when people ask me."

"So no one asks you anymore."

He pressed his lips together. "So it would seem."

"What did Sarah think of your honesty?"

"Sarah demanded honesty," Reynolds said, perking up at the mention of her name. "If you didn't like a piece or a series, she wanted to hear it in plain language. No waffling around or trying to be nice."

"So the two of you got along well."

"Her work was better than Isaac's. I can't say I understand what all of the fuss was about. I don't think it was brilliant or inspired. But she would tell me that wasn't what she was going for."

"What did she think of the way that you critiqued other artists' work?"

Reynolds took another drink. "Like I said, she prized honesty."

"She told you that you should be brutally honest about *other* artists' work?"

"No, not exactly."

"What did she think about how you ripped into Lewis Riley back in the day?"

Reynolds shook his head. "I don't remember the name. Sorry."

"One of the men you went to art school with. He is now homeless, living in Inglewood or Pearce Estate Park. Sarah had run into him and recognized him. She must have told you about it."

"No. Why would she tell me about it?"

"Because she blamed you for destroying his artistic career, maybe resulting in his homelessness. You took his future away. I would be very surprised if she had said *nothing* to you about it."

Reynolds shrugged and didn't protest, but his meaning

was obvious. He still was not admitting that he had talked to Sarah about it.

"If that's all you have, Detective, I have other work to do."

"And then you talked to Violet. And she told you about the new series Sarah was working on. A man whose life and art you had destroyed and who lived in the park, picking bottles."

"I had no idea of any of that."

"I don't believe that."

"Well…" He shook his head. "I can't help what you believe. If you don't know the truth when you hear it…"

"It's amazing the technology we have at our disposal these days, isn't it?" Margie asked, unlocking her screen and looking down at her phone.

Reynolds looked at her. "What do you mean?"

"I mean, you can call each other, text messages back and forth, even pictures or videos."

He gulped and said nothing.

"And at the park, they used to have a lot more issues with security, but that has been reduced since they put up cameras in the parking lot. They're everywhere now; you don't even see them. But if you are on your way to confront or possibly kill someone, you really should keep your eyes open."

He turned a pasty gray. He held the cup to his mouth but couldn't seem to drink.

"I don't understand," he finally croaked.

"You don't have an alibi, but we actually do know where you were before Sarah's accident."

Margie turned her phone around to let him look at it. A nicely framed picture of him walking through the parking lot at Pearce Estate Park.

CHAPTER TWENTY-TWO

*R*eynolds stared at the picture on Margie's phone. Sweat broke out on his temples, though his face remained smooth and impassive.

"I don't know where or when that was taken," he said, with only a slight quaver in his voice.

"Of course you do," Margie told him, in a calm, reassuring voice. "You realized that Sarah's new series of paintings was about *you*. That it would reveal what you had done to Lewis and others. That people would find out about you stealing and copying other artists' work. You spent all of this time building up your reputation and fighting for recognition, and she was threatening to take it all away from you."

"She was such a hypocrite!" Reynolds exploded. "She acted like she was so much better than anyone else, that she was educating the public about social issues that we all needed to be aware of and work to abolish. It's easy to see what's wrong when you look at what everyone else is doing. Yes, we have poverty and addiction and mental illness and all of those other things that she was so intent on 'exposing.' But what can I do about that? As an individual, what can I really do?"

Margie nodded encouragingly.

"She advocated for programs for the homeless and supporting people at poverty wages. All while she lived in that monstrosity. She decides she's going to ruin me because of something that happened years ago to Lewis? Someone she hadn't even bothered to keep track of? What right does she have to be judge and jury and destroy my life?"

"You just wanted to talk to her," Margie suggested.

"I didn't go there to hurt anyone," he insisted. "I wanted her to see what she was doing, to be reasonable. What good would it do to ruin me? How would that help Lewis? If she wanted to help him, why didn't she give him money? Or a job? Why didn't she invite him to stay in that mansion of hers? She lived alone. Violet didn't live in. Sarah broke up with Jonathan and kicked him out. She was all by herself in that huge mansion that could have housed thirty immigrant families. If she felt bad about Lewis, then why didn't she do something about it?"

"No one could change what had happened in the past," Margie agreed, careful to keep passive voice. Not what Reynolds had done to Lewis but what had happened to Lewis. No accusation, no hint of responsibility.

"No," Reynolds agreed. "That's exactly right. Ruining me wouldn't change Lewis's situation. What would it achieve? She would be able to stop anyone from getting their feelings hurt in the future? She would change the face of the art community? Her paintings were not going to change anything."

"Except for you. You were afraid that people would identify who it was that she was painting about, and that they would turn on you."

"What does it matter what I did back in school? When

we were all still starting out? This isn't something that I did last week. I was a stupid kid, I'll admit that. I didn't know how to handle myself. But it isn't all on me." He looked affronted, as if Margie had accused him unjustly. "People have to make their own choices in life and to live with them. Lewis didn't have to leave art. He didn't have to make whatever other choices he made to end up on the street. He could have done what the rest of us did, working at it and struggling and finding a way to pull ourselves up and get what we wanted. It's not my fault that he made the choices he did."

"Actually," Margie said, "Lewis isn't really homeless. He's an undercover cop. He decided to go into law enforcement. He's only living on the streets temporarily as part of his cover."

Reynolds's mouth dropped open. He looked at Margie in horror. At first, she didn't understand why he felt so strongly about it. But she followed the logical progression. He had killed Sarah because she was painting a series that exposed his past and his unethical or illegal practices. Sarah had chosen to paint the series because she had seen Lewis living on the street and in the park and sought some kind of justice for what had been done to him back in art school. But Lewis wasn't a broken man living on the streets because Reynolds had destroyed all of his dreams. It was just an act. Reynolds had done what he had for no reason at all.

"Tell me about how the conversation with Sarah went," Margie prompted him.

It was a difficult barrier for him to cross. He had as much as admitted that he had been there. That he had hurt Lewis in the past. That he was angry with Sarah for trying to ruin him for no good reason. But if he were to recount the conversation with Sarah Thompson, he would have to admit what he had done to her.

Was there a way out of it? Could he just keep denying it?

His best bet was to just tell Margie what had happened. She would see that he had been justified in what he had done. He would be able to shed his burden and they would find a way to move on. Someone would understand and he wouldn't have to keep hiding, worried that every call was going to be someone who had figured out his secret.

He had held on to a lot of secrets in the past. Maybe that was the way to connect with him.

"What happened in school happened a long time ago," Margie said.

He nodded eagerly. "Yes. It was a lifetime ago. I was a different person then. Do I regret that Lewis took my words so personally and decided not to pursue a career in art?" He considered his own question seriously. "I guess that on one hand I regret it. I would never want to harm anyone. But on the other hand, I didn't say anything that wasn't true. And he could have chosen to just work harder. To listen to someone else's opinion instead of mine. They were writing nice things about him in the paper. Why not focus on that instead of on a few throw-away comments that I made?"

"I don't know if that's what made him leave art," Margie said generously. "Who knows. He may just have decided that it wasn't for him. It's not an easy scene to break into, is it?"

"No. It's not. And not everybody is cut out for it. He probably decided that he needed a regular paycheck. Living as a creative is extremely difficult, and I went through a lot of lean years before I managed to break through the barriers."

"You struggled with other areas too. He might have been more talented than you, who is to say? But you had to pay your dues too. You had to deal with not having your own particular style, but borrowing from others instead. You had to figure out how to make that work. There were a lot of detractors. A lot of people who wanted to keep you down. Laws and rules of ethics that were murky and contradictory."

Reynolds nodded. "Why is it okay to copy the old masters, but not anyone more current? Why is copying a valid learning method, but only to a certain degree? When is following someone else's style valid and encouraged and when does it cross the line into copying or derivative works or art plagiarism? There is no clear line."

"It wasn't like you were trying to do anything unethical. You were only trying to build up your catalog, to be noticed. To find a way to make a living."

"It seems like it is so easy for some people," Reynolds complained. "They just walk right into it and everyone welcomes them with open arms, like Sarah. And someone like me, who has just as much talent as she does, is kept down. I have to keep struggling against these arbitrary rules about what is creative and what is copying."

"It must have been very frustrating. You just wanted to explain that to Sarah."

"Yes. I wanted to tell her that I was just doing what I had to do to succeed. And that what had happened to Lewis all those years ago… it wasn't my fault. She needed to just back off and leave me alone."

His words at the end were stronger, angrier. He was working himself back up into a self-justified, righteous anger. Margie could use that.

"So you knew she was going to be at the park. Maybe Violet told you. And you went there to discuss it with her. Away from offices where others might overhear you and misinterpret what was being said. Away from all of the pressures and distractions, people wanting to be involved in what was none of their business."

"I'm not a big nature buff," Reynolds confessed. "I like landscapes, but I'm not someone who needs to walk outside in the dust and the smog to regenerate. But I thought that if I could see her there, I could explain it all. I could convince her that what she was doing was pointless and would just hurt more people."

Margie nodded.

Reynolds looked like he was expecting her to guess the rest of the story for him, but Margie just sat there, waiting. He had started his tale. If she didn't say anything, he would need to fill the silence. He'd gone too far to just stop and not explain himself now.

"I followed her to that place, the campsite beside the railway tracks. She said that I needed to grow up and stand on my own two feet."

He shook his head, the movements tight and angry. "Stand on my own two feet! Grow up! I am just as much an adult as she is. Was. She said if I was a man, I'd be able to take my own medicine. Actions have consequences." He growled, a wordless, feral sound. "Well, her actions had consequences too. She couldn't just paint whatever she felt like when it affects someone else. Isn't that what all of those civil rights people are always saying? Your right to swing your fist ends where my nose begins? You can't harm other people. That's going too far. And here she was, ready to destroy me completely. She didn't have the right!"

"You felt like it was a personal attack."

"It was!" Reynolds agreed, his voice going up. "That's exactly what it was. A personal attack. I had the right to defend myself."

"And how did you do that?"

"I told her that I wasn't going to let her finish the paintings. She mouthed off about how I couldn't stop her, blah blah blah. She told me to go away or she would call the cops. Did she think that they would come? That she could tell me I was trespassing when she didn't own the property? You can't make someone else leave a public place just because you feel like it. She didn't own it."

Margie nodded and waited for him to go on.

"She tried to push me away, back toward the pathway. Told me to leave her alone, that I couldn't stop her from expressing herself, from 'educating' everyone as to what kind of a person I really was. She said I had no talent," his tone was outraged, "and that everything I had ever created was a copy of someone else's work. And that's not true!"

He nursed his anger for a short time, breathing heavily. "I shoved her back. She laid hands on me, I had the right to defend myself. She fell over backwards. Fat old broad had had zero athletic abilities. Just keeled over when I barely even touched her." He apparently decided that "shoved" was too aggressive a word. "And... she hit her head."

"And...?" Margie prompted, when he didn't continue. Reynolds surely had a cell phone to call for help. He could run back to the pathway where there were other people, get someone to help him with first aid. The usual reaction to someone falling down and hitting her head was not to drag her to the railway track and leave her there.

Reynolds shook his head. "She didn't move. She didn't get up. I checked, but I didn't think she had a pulse or was breathing. There was nothing I could do then. It was just an accident. And I didn't really push her, I just, you know..." Reynolds demonstrated a small, gentle movement in the air, "It wasn't my fault."

"Where did she fall? What did she hit her head on?"

"I don't know. A rock, I guess. I didn't know what to do. I just... got out of there."

"Was she on the railway tracks when you left?"

He swallowed. "I guess she was."

"So if she wasn't dead from the fall, you intended to kill her with the train?"

"No, that wasn't the way it was... I just... there wasn't anything I could do, so I got out of there."

"I see." Margie stood up. "Well, you're under arrest, Mr. Reynolds. If you'll please stand. We'll get you booked."

CHAPTER TWENTY-THREE

$\mathcal{M}$argie's phone had rung several times while she had been interviewing Reynolds and getting him taken care of. Now that Reynolds was out of the way, Margie had to focus on typing her reports and ensuring that his recorded interview confession was properly linked in the workspace. Once that was done, she supposed MacDonald would want to have a small press conference or, at least, issue a press release and call one of the papers to let them know that Sarah Thompson's killer had been arrested. It would make a big splash, considering that up until today, the media had been told that it appeared to be a tragic accident and nothing else. Margie wasn't sure what time she would be able to go home.

But she knew that at least one of her missed calls had been from Christina, so as soon as she sat down at her desk, she looked at the display on her phone and saw that Christina had called not just once, but several times.

Her stomach clenched. She always tried to get back to Christina as quickly as possible, but sometimes she couldn't leave what she was doing. Was there a problem at school? Or worse, with Moushoom? Margie had thought it was a good idea for Christina to be able to talk to the nursing home about Moushoom's condition whenever she wanted to, but what if he had taken a downturn and Christina had no one to talk to about it?

Margie immediately tapped Christina's name on her call log.

"Christina?" she spoke as soon as the call connected. "I'm sorry I couldn't answer right away. Is everything okay?"

"Oh, Mom." Christina's voice sounded a little wobbly. Margie held her breath; the phone clenched in her hand so tightly it would take a crowbar to pry it out. "I called to see how Moushoom was doing."

Margie's worst fear. He had gotten worse. Had they taken him to the hospital? Had they made the wrong choice and waited too long, and now it was too late for the hospital to do anything? She thought of the pictures she had seen of gurneys lining the halls of the hospital.

"What did they say?" she asked, trying to keep her voice steady.

"They took him off of oxygen."

Margie gulped. Did Christina mean they had removed all support and were just going to let him go? She had told them to do everything possible for him.

"They what?"

"He's doing better. He's getting enough oxygen without the machine. They said that his pneumonia is clearing up. They might put him back on oxygen at night; they're going to watch his numbers and see how he does."

Margie let out a sob of relief. "Oh, that's really good news, sweetie. Thank you for letting me know. They think he's on the mend, then."

"Yeah. They got his COVID test back, and they said it

was negative. It was bacterial, and the antibiotic is clearing it up."

Margie had been worrying about long COVID and the possibility of permanent lung and heart damage. Now she could let that worry go too.

"Wonderful. Oh, I'm so glad to hear that. Did you tell them to say we love him and miss him?"

"Yes. He might be able to have visitors in a day or two, as long as the facility doesn't go on lockdown."

It would be good to see him again. She looked forward to telling him all about the case that had begun with their walk in Pearce Estate Park.

She was sure he would find it interesting.

PEARCE ESTATE PARK

Pearce Estate Park is a 21-hectare natural haven nestled in a curve of the Bow River in southeast Calgary, seamlessly blending urban convenience with serene wildlife and plant life. The park features reconstructed wetlands, ponds, and streams that support a diverse range of plant species such as willows, Water Birch, and cattails.

Nature enthusiasts can enjoy birdwatching with species like White-breasted Nuthatches and Northern Flickers making frequent appearances. Families will appreciate the play-grounds and open spaces perfect for picnics or leisurely strolls along well-maintained pathways. Additionally, the adjacent Bow Habitat Station offers an immersive experience into aquatic ecosystems through its Sam Livingston Fish Hatchery Visitor Centre.

The author has spent many hours in Pearce Estate Park, beginning with when she and her husband were dating and gathered with other young adults for a fire and songs accompanied by guitar. She also went on numerous nature walks there with her son and frequently watched a medieval re-enactment group sword fighting.

Did you enjoy this book? Reviews and recommendations are vital to making a book successful.

Please leave a review at your favorite book store or review site and share it with your friends.

Don't miss the following bonus material:
Sign up for mailing list to get a free bonus
Read a sneak preview chapter
Other books by P.D. Workman
Learn more about the author

Get the Parks Pat Survival Pack!

Sign up for my newsletter and receive the **exclusive Parks Pat Survival Pack**, packed with bonus materials and extra goodies you won't find anywhere else.

Stay in the loop on new releases, special offers, and insider content—all delivered straight to your inbox.

Sign up today and start your adventure with Parks Pat!

https://shop.pdworkman.com/products/parks-pat-survival-pack

Here's what's inside:
• Out with the Sunset (Book 1, eBook)
Begin Margie's journey with her first gripping case as a Calgary homicide officer in the Parks Pat Mysteries.

- **Out with the Sunset (Book 1, Audiobook – Computer Narrated)**

Take the mystery on the go—perfect for your commute, workout, or a walk through the park.

- **Bonus Prequel Story:** *Flight of the Bluejay*

Discover Margie's *true beginning*. Before she was a sleuth, she was a pregnant teen on the streets—fighting to survive and find her place in the world.

- **Discover Calgary's Treasures – Photo Minibook**

Step into the beauty of Calgary with this exclusive photo album showcasing the first 15 parks that inspired the series.

- **Digital Wallpapers**

Bring the beauty of Calgary's parks to your phone, tablet, or computer with stunning photography.

SNEAK PEEK AT BENCH
WITH A VIEW

BENCH WITH A VIEW

Sitting on a Deadly Secret

A body on a park bench looks peaceful—too peaceful. Detective Margie "Parks Pat" Patenaude quickly realizes the woman didn't die there. She was posed. Now Margie must untangle the motive behind this chilling display and track down a killer who is sending a message.

The deeper she digs, the closer the case cuts to home, testing both her investigative skills and her personal strength. Some secrets refuse to stay buried, and Margie will have to face them head-on before another life is lost.

Tropes You'll Love:
    1 a suspiciously staged crime scene,
    2 clever detective work,
    3 psychological suspense,
    4 personal stakes for the hero, and
    5 a brisk, satisfying police procedural.

☆☆☆☆☆ "For me, this is the best story yet in a fine series that consistently offers intriguing police procedural mysteries from the perspective of a female Métis detective dedicated to her profession, her family, and her culture."

Take a walk with Parks Pat—hold onto your seat for this suspenseful story!

CHAPTER ONE

*M*argie really didn't like early morning calls.

The sunrise was so late in the autumn and winter that she really couldn't expect the sun to have risen before she got to every homicide site. But she never could understand people getting up so early to run or walk their dogs, coming across fresh bodies when it was still too early for Margie to drag herself out of bed.

She had been doing better about getting out to run before work herself but, sometimes, she just kept snoozing her alarms until it was too late to get out. She had stumbled across a body herself on one of her early-morning runs, so who was she to criticize anyone else for doing the same thing?

Margie sat up and grabbed her phone from the nightstand. She used her thumb to answer the call and held it to her ear.

"Patenaude."

"I'm looking for Parks Pat," the dispatcher told her cheerfully.

"This is Detective Pat," she acknowledged, trying not to groan. "Does that mean you've got a body in a park?"

"Carburn Park this morning. DB on a park bench."

Margie envisioned a homeless person sleeping on a bench and dying from hypothermia overnight. It had been a mild fall so far, but Calgary weather was not kind to those who preferred to sleep rough.

She covered a yawn before speaking again. "Where is Carburn Park?"

"Not far from you, actually. But it's one of those little gems that is kind of tucked away, and you don't know about it unless it's in your neighborhood or someone tells you about it."

"Okay." Margie cleared her throat. She picked up the water bottle from the nightstand and had a drink. She was not an early-morning person. "I will punch it into my GPS and get there as soon as I can. Tell them I'm on my way."

"Will do, detective."

"Has OCME been called?"

"Yes. They will be behind you. I'm not sure how long you'll have to wait. Take coffee."

"Okay. Thanks."

Margie didn't need to terminate the call; the dispatcher had already hung up. Margie rubbed her eyes. She knew better than to lie back down or even just sit on the edge of the bed waiting until she was fully awake. It was a sure way to fall back asleep.

She went to the bathroom to splash water on her face and quickly do her hair, coiling her long braid on top of her head. She didn't start the coffee machine in the kitchen. It might wake up Christina. Instead, she would stop by Tim's and get a box of coffee for herself and the other professionals already on the scene. She had learned that the Take 12 worked better than taking a tray of filled cups, when she could only carry a few at a time.

"Mom?"

Margie stopped in Christina's bedroom doorway as she left the bathroom.

"Go back to sleep, honey. It's not time yet."

"You got a call?"

"Yeah."

"I'll call you when I get up."

"That would be great. Let me know how you are doing."

Christina murmured a reply and fell back asleep. They had agreed that Margie would not wake her up before leaving when she was called out, but often Christina woke up anyway when she heard Margie getting ready. Christina would get the details when she was up and getting ready for school or riding the bus.

Stella, though, was a different story. However excited the dog was when Margie got home from work or took her for a walk in the morning, she did not stir if Margie got up before seven—a dog after Margie's own heart.

CHAPTER TWO

*W*ith her Take 12 in the footwell of the passenger seat, Margie set up Carburn Park on her GPS and headed out. The electronic voice directed her south on Deerfoot Trail, which was busier than Margie would have expected so early in the morning. But at least she didn't have to contend with rush hour traffic. The drivers of the cars out on the road were happy to let her zoom over the Calf Robe Bridge and down to Glenmore, even without flashing lights.

She didn't need emergency lights or siren to get to a homicide scene. What difference would it make if she arrived five minutes later without a siren? The victim was already dead. The Office of the Chief Medical Examiner death scene investigator would be behind her somewhere, and the other crime scene investigators wouldn't have much reason to be there before it was light and they could see what they were doing properly. It wasn't like a kidnapping or hostage situation where seconds counted. The victim would still be dead when she arrived.

What had looked like a fairly simple route to the park

turned out to be a lot of twists and turns, and then, finally, Margie reached the park entrance.

It was right in the middle of a residential area. Probably a lot of walkers liked to take their turn around the park every day or two. Lots of witnesses who could help narrow down the time of death. Though there had probably been only a few walkers out that late or early.

Margie drove in slowly and parked her car with a cluster of other vehicles. A young constable with a traffic wand indicated the direction she should go. "Around the pond here, ma'am. Clockwise is shorter. Just keep hugging the pond on your right. Can't miss it."

Margie could see large lights being set up partway around the pond. She would have to be blind to miss them. "Thank you," she told him and offered the Tim's box. He took a cup and she filled it.

"Thank you!" he said, pulling down his mask to drink and giving her an appreciative grin.

Margie switched the box of coffee from one side to the other as she walked around the pond. It wasn't that heavy, but it got heavier the farther she walked.

As she approached, she studied the scene, brightly lit in the middle of the dark park. It was a strange sight, like a play or tableau with spotlights on it. She had imagined an old man in voluminous coats lying on the park bench, having passed away in his sleep. Not too much to investigate. Just a natural death. Sad, but something that inevitably happened at least once a year in Calgary, usually in the depths of winter when it was 35 or 40 below. Some homeless person sitting in a bus shelter to avoid the wind and snow.

Instead, the victim appeared to be sitting up. As if he were just looking out onto the pond and had fallen asleep, never to wake up again.

As Margie got closer and again switched the Tim's Take

12 from one hand to the other, she realized the victim was a woman rather than a man.

It didn't take long to reach the bench. At her approach, the other law enforcement officers looked up and fell silent. Margie stopped a short distance away to put on protective gear. She wasn't as sure now that it was just someone who had died of hypothermia or passed away in her sleep.

"Here, someone better take this," Margie offered, showing the Tim's coffee. A couple of officers hurried to take it from her and set it on a table with folding legs that had been set up away from the scene. Margie saw a garbage bag that already contained a few discarded coffee cups.

Free of her offering, Margie approached the bench to have a look at the victim.

It looked at first glance as though the woman were merely sleeping on the bench. Her face was at rest, her eyes closed. Her body was leaning slightly to the side but not falling over. As if she might jerk awake at any moment. The bright white lights were not flattering, but she did not have the gray pallor of many of the victims Margie saw. Her skin was a rich golden brown and had not yet taken on the chalkiness Margie expected. She was probably around Margie's age, in her thirties, and was not a homeless person. Her hair and skin were well-cared-for and her overcoat was pristine and good quality. Margie couldn't see the brand and didn't know enough about fashion to immediately identify it, but guessed it was LL Bean or a pricier brand.

"Well, this is not at all what I was expecting," she told the others.

"What were you expecting?" one of the patrol cops asked, taking a sip of the fresh Tim's coffee.

"The dispatcher said a body on a park bench, and I just figured… an old homeless man."

"That'll teach you not to jump to conclusions."

"Do we have a name yet? Does anyone know how long she's been here?"

"No identification yet. But we haven't touched anything other than to make sure that she was dead. Waiting on you and the ME's office."

Margie was not going to go poking through the woman's pockets either. She would wait until the death investigator had a chance to examine the body in situ and to check her pockets and handbag.

"Does she have a purse?" Margie asked, looking around.

Everyone looked at the woman, under the bench, and scanned the nearby ground.

"Nothing immediately obvious. We'll need to check the bushes and water when it's light out."

"Yeah." Margie took another step back and carefully looked around. There was no sign of the woman's personal possessions. "Is she wearing any jewelry? Watch?"

"You think it was a mugging? Doesn't look like any mugging I've ever seen," disagreed a cop with a short, grizzled beard that showed around his mask.

"No, I'm not making any assumptions. I'm in the information-gathering phase."

Margie stretched medical gloves over her warm gloves and gently pushed back the sleeves and collar of the coat to expose the victim's wrists and throat.

She was wearing a pretty but practical wristwatch. It was not a big name, nothing Margie recognized, and probably the jewels inset in the bezel were nothing more than zircons. No wedding ring on her finger. No necklace.

"No gloves," the younger cop noted.

Margie nodded. "It might be unseasonably warm, but I still wouldn't walk to this side of the pond without gloves, much less sit down to watch the ducks or wait for someone to meet me with bare hands."

She had made sure she had her gloves on before she stepped out of her car and picked up the Tim's box. Had the woman walked over and sat down without gloves? If so, why? Had it been a rush trip and she'd forgotten? Had she dropped them? Had someone taken them? With a jacket like that, she had to have gloves. Probably leather. Real leather, not the synthetic stuff.

Margie made a mental note of the missing purse and gloves. She didn't want to take off her own gloves to write in her notebook yet; it seemed like it took forever for her fingers to warm up again once they'd gotten good and cold. Policing in the cold weather was not at the top of her list of favorite things to do—especially middle-of-the-night or early-morning callouts.

Bench With a View, Book #11 of the *Parks Pat Mysteries*
series by P.D. Workman
can be purchased at pdworkman.com or at your favorite
online retailers

ABOUT THE AUTHOR

P.D. Workman is a USA Today Bestselling author and multi-award winner, renowned for her prolific output of over 100 published works that span various genres. With a knack for crafting page-turners, Workman captivates readers with everything from cozy mysteries like the Auntie Clem's Bakery series to gripping young adult and suspense novels.

A prolific reader and writer since childhood, P.D. Workman crafts emotionally powerful stories that don't shy away from hard topics. Her books tackle mental illness, addiction, abuse, and trauma with raw honesty and compassion, giving voice to the often unheard. If you crave authentic, character-driven page-turners that hit deep and stay with you long after the final page, you're in the right place.

With each new release, fans eagerly anticipate another thrilling blend of thought-provoking storytelling and relatable characters that define P.D. Workman's brand as an author of unforgettable page-turners—gripping tales that leave a lasting impact long after the last page is turned.

> P. D. Workman, does not shy from probing the deep psychological scars of childhood trauma, mental illness, and addiction. Also characteristic of this author, these extremely sensitive issues are explored with extensive empathy, described with incredible clarity, and portrayed with profound insight.

Some of Workman's titles have been translated into Spanish, French, Portuguese, German, and Italian.

Workman began writing at an early age and is a prolific reader as well as writer. She is also passionate about teaching and learning, expresses her creativity through art and cooking, and loves exploring the Calgary parks and green spaces where the Parks Pat Mysteries are set. She was a legal assistant for many years and has done extensive charitable work.

Workman was born and raised in Alberta, Canada, and is married with one adult son.

Please visit P.D. Workman at pdworkman.com to see what else she is working on, to join her mailing list, and to link to her social networks.

If you enjoyed this book, please take the time to recommend it to other purchasers with a review or star rating and share it with your friends!

tiktok.com/@pdworkmanauthor

facebook.com/pdworkmanauthor

x.com/pdworkmanauthor

instagram.com/pdworkmanauthor

amazon.com/author/pdworkman

bookbub.com/authors/p-d-workman

goodreads.com/pdworkman

linkedin.com/in/pdworkman

pinterest.com/pdworkmanauthor

youtube.com/pdworkman

Find P.D. Workman's books at

PDWORKMAN.COM

Scan the QR code below